7:40

IAN GRANT

IAN GRANT
22 Cloughley Dr.
Barrie. ON L4N 7Y3
(705) 726-9677

Pigtails, Petticoats and the Old School Tie

D0869647

Overseas Missionary Fellowship
1058 Avenue Road
Toronto, Ontario M5N 2C6

Books by the same author

The Shark's Fin Five
Tara
My Book about Hudson
I went to School . . . in the Jungle

Sheila Miller

PIGTAILS, PETTICOATS AND THE OLD SCHOOL TIE

To my mother, who loves children
and showed me how to do the same

OMF BOOKS

© OVERSEAS MISSIONARY FELLOWSHIP
(formerly China Inland Mission)
First printed 1981

ISBN 0 85363 140 9

Cover design and artwork by Jon N. Miller

Published by Overseas Missionary Fellowship
Belmont, The Vine, SEVENOAKS, Kent, TN13 3TZ.

Printed in Great Britain by A. Wheaton & Co., Ltd., Exeter

CONTENTS

	Page
Foreword by James H. Taylor III	7
Preface	11
Question Marks	13
The Lads for whom he died	19
Yentai	23
Slow Train Coming	25
Shoes and Ships	41
Driftwood	49
A Spoonful of Sugar . . .	67
Mortar Board and Gown	77
Did you hear the one about . . .	85
Thorn Bushes have Roses	99
String of Pearls	123
When Icicles hang by the Wall	127
Goodbye Chefoo	137
Both sides of the Hump	167
The Fall of the Bamboo Curtain	179
Yentai today	197
And the Wheels go on turning	201

'I am recording this
   so that future generations
will also praise the Lord
   for all that He has done'.

Psalm 102.8 (Living Bible)

FOREWORD

by James H Taylor III, OMF General Director, Chefusian 1937–1945

How is it possible for missionaries to pursue their calling without undue interruption and for their children to receive a sound education without long and harmful separations? That is what Chefoo is all about.

One hundred years ago an idea was translated into action, vision became reality, and Chefoo was born. Our beloved school song of an earlier period describes it more aptly: a lamp was lit on the shores of an eastern sea. Now for a century the sons and daughters of dedicated missionary parents have passed under the glow of that lamp. As a result their lives, their families and the world have all in turn been enriched.

To provide an education in China for missionaries' children at the close of the 19th century must have seemed like an idle dream indeed. Conservative forces in the Ching Dynasty were even then rallying for what proved to be their last stand. In less than twenty years vast areas of North China would erupt in the insanity of the Boxer Rebellion, only to be followed by five decades of relentless revolutionary struggle.

It was against such a turbulent backdrop that the China Inland Mission schools were started in Chefoo. During these one hundred years, while nearly every country in East Asia and indeed the CIM itself has each gone through its own respective metamorphosis, the lamp that was lit at Chefoo has continued to burn.

Today Chefoo is not just a place. It is a concept. The original Chefoo school may no longer exist, but its ethos, as Sheila Miller has so poignantly described, was carried from China overseas. The 'Chefoo' concept is rather beautifully expressed by a clause from each of the three verses of the original school song.

'Storing our minds' speaks of a commitment to excellence in education . . . 'to Latin, French and history; and to scientific mystery; to geography, geometry . . .' In China days the distinguished record in Oxford matriculation exemption exams gives testimony to the reality of Chefoo's academic commitment.

'To conquer a friendly foe' brings to mind the amazing variety of competitive sports that children at Chefoo enjoy. In my own day, the pennant in the 'Prep' and the shield in the Boys' School were coveted awards won by only the very few, but for almost everyone there was a chance to participate in cricket, football and hockey; track events of every kind, including the long run; swimming, rowing and tennis. Individual as well as house (Carey, Livingstone, Morrison and Paton) rivalry was always very keen and utterly wholesome.

'Set we a nobler aim' expresses Chefoo's unapologetic recognition of a spiritual dimension in life where God's glory is man's highest aim. The Prep School motto, 'Remember Jesus Christ', and the swelling anthem, 'Lord of all power and might, Who art the Author and Giver of all good things . . .', that brought Memorial Day celebrations to a quiet climax were part of a larger, carefully-planned educational experience for the whole person. The Sunday morning worship at the Port Churches, or the school services in Memorial Hall, helped many a student to lay a sound foundation for life.

All of us Chefusians are indebted to Sheila Miller for the long hours of painstaking effort she has spent in research and writing the Chefoo story. This is not merely a historical record, it is also a tremendous testimony to the faithfulness of God. I am confident that it will help many a reader to draw afresh on the spiritual resources that have constituted such an integral part of Chefoo past and present.

8

CHEFOO SCHOOL SONG

Greet we the School in whose honour we sing,
Whose fame is our trust and care!
Grateful affection to thee would we bring,
Proof by the deeds we dare.
Storing our minds with the lore of the past;
Secrets of Nature's Art;
Fresh conquests making, we strive to the last
Nobly to play our part.

Under the glow of a lamp that is lit
On the shores of an Eastern sea;
Daughters and sons, in loyalty knit,
Plight we our troth to thee.

Stung by the icy blasts of the North,
Or jaded with South-wind blow,
Team against team to battle goes forth
To conquer a friendly foe.
Riding the billows we rise and fall,
Straining with rhythmic swing;
Partners, we serve and return the ball,
Swift as a stone from a sling.

Under the glow of a lamp . . .

Plaudits of men we lightly appraise,
Set we a nobler aim —
Ever to bring through the toil of the days
Glory to GOD'S great Name.
Many the voices that ring in our ears,
Many the cries of need;
God give us grace in the coming years
His voice alone to heed.

Plaudits of men we lightly appraise,
Set we a nobler aim —
Ever to bring through the toil of the days
Glory to GOD'S great Name.

CHRONOLOGY

1879	Purchase of 'beanfield', East Beach, Chefoo
1881	The birth of the 'Protestant Collegiate School' of the CIM, Port of Chefoo, China
1896	Foundation Stone of new building laid
1900	Boxer Rising in China
1901	Food poisoning incident, resulting in 13 deaths at school
1906	Master's drowning accident
1911	Bubonic Plague hit Port of Chefoo
1914–18	First World War when 34 'old boys' gave their lives
1923–24	Memorial Hall built to commemorate those who died in the war
1934	Co-ed building erected
1935	Piracy
1937	Start of Sino-Japanese War
1939–45	Second World War
1941	Pearl Harbour
1941	Emergency Prep School formed in Kiating
1942	Chefoo School transferred to Weihsien Internment Camp
1944	Evacuation of Kiating for Kalimpong
1946	Chefoo School transferred to Shanghai
1947	Chefoo School transferred to Kuling on the River Yangtse
1951	Evacuation of China
1951	Chefoo School, Japan opened
1952	Small prep school started in Bangkok
1954	Chefoo School, Malaysia opened
1954	Chefoo School, Philippines opened
1981	Chefoo School, Philippines closed
1981	Chefoo School's Centennial Year

PREFACE

Our family lived for eight years at Chefoo School in the jungle of Malaysia, where my husband was headmaster, our son had his own early years of schooling and I was a teacher. And ever since we arrived home in Britain in 1979 I've still been living in Chefoo, immersed in thoughts of the old school of China days and our delightful memories of Chefoo today.

Six years ago we circulated hundreds of questionnaires among Chefusians of bygone days, to uncover their recollections. The global response was tremendous — filled-in forms, closely-written sheets of reminiscences, ancient diaries, photographs, sketches, old magazines, cuttings from newspapers, manuscripts and even cassette tapes. I felt totally inadequate for the assignment OMF had asked me to undertake — the history book of Chefoo's hundred years. Bishop Frank Houghton summed up my trepidation in these lovely words:

'It is a secret joy
To find
The task assigned
Beyond our powers,
For then, if ought of good be wrought,
Clearly the praise is His
Not ours.'

But without all my contributors, this Chefoo saga could never have been written. I specially want to thank every single person who has made this book possible. Chefoo means people . . . Chefusians with a story to tell. Did the school really continue in Japanese internment camp? Were 74 Chefoo pupils actually captured by real-life pirates on the South China Sea as Peter Pan had been by Captain Hook? That girl who fell off the train — did she live? The

11

tales run the gamut of childhood's carefree smiles and homesick tears. Memories are here, worldwide memories, triggered by the magic of a name — Chefoo.

Yet this anthology of the Chefoo Schools is relevant to folk other than the variety called 'missionaries' — to those, perhaps, who have queries about Christian work abroad. Should a missionary send his child away to boarding school or not? It is my hope that readers will come to a new appreciation of what separation costs the missionary family, yet also of how so many missionaries and their children experience the 'hundredfold' blessing promised by the Lord in such circumstances.

One old girl concluded her own narrative with the question, 'Will there be time to get your book out before the Rapture?' Frankly, at times I wondered myself, but Centennial Year has arrived and here the book is! In this special year of celebration gatherings, it's good to think of the gigantic Chefoo reunion there will be when the Lord does come back.

My prayer is that in this book you will find new slants of truth about the Saviour and a new understanding of missionaries' children, and that God will bless each one of you richly.

Sheila P. Miller
February 1981

QUESTION MARKS

Hudson Taylor

Mr Taylor was ill.

Mr Hudson Taylor that was. The man who had the panoramic vision of reaching every province in China for the Lord Jesus . . . the man who had started the China Inland Mission. To convalesce he was sent to a healthy spot on the shores of the Yellow Sea — a port with a name that today sparks off memories like spray flung far along the China coast. Chefoo.

On that sandy beach an idea was born.

Chefoo — a bracing opportunity for other tired missionaries to regain their strength? Chefoo — a perfect location for a school for missionaries' children? These question marks challenged Mr Taylor's faith. Faced with problems, he used to say that three phases accompanied most great tasks undertaken for God! Impossible. Difficult. Done!

How like God to give new plans amid sickness, sifting purpose from seemingly wasted days, building dreams through difficulties. Castles in the air have a promise of reality when God is the architect.

Yes! A school. That's what was needed. How else could Roger in far-distant Kansu be prepared for a career in America? How else could Marjory, living four months' travel inland, in the province of Szechwan, have a British education?

Few alternatives came up. A local school, near the parents' mission station? Sometimes. But they did their mathematics in Chinese. Send the children back to Britain or the States? What parents could feel happy about sending a little six-year-old so far away? Those were the days when correspondence courses hadn't been thought of. Yet would that be an answer? How would a growing child fare socially?

A special China Inland Mission School where teaching in English was provided, where preparing children for tertiary education at home was priority — that was the best solution.

Where? How? With what? The seaport of Chefoo seemed an ideal location. But the China Inland Mission had nowhere to build in Chefoo. Obtaining land in China was difficult. Mr Taylor gazed longingly at the hills where a secluded spot with nicely rising ground offered an attractive situation . . . So near the beach, too, with a little freshwater stream running down to the shore. It wouldn't be good to show interest in that field, though. The farmer who owned the field might notice, and quote a price which the mission could never meet. Mr Taylor and his friend, Mr Judd, only prayed.

Yet, one day . . . How many stories have that thrilling once-upon-a-time start! No wonder Chefoo School has always loved that special name for God — 'Jehovah Jireh — the Lord will provide.' Watch how He did it.

One day Mr Taylor and Mr Judd were walking across that particular field. 'Are you interested in buying land?' Surprised by the Chinese voice, they halted abruptly. Had he overheard their English conversation? How could he possibly know that they had just been discussing the possibilities of this field, as a site?

'Do you want land?' repeated the farmer.

With little apparent interest, they said they *might* like to buy some.

'Then, will you buy mine?'

He was offering that very bean field!

'How much?'

A reasonable price!

'Then and there the bargain was struck', exclaimed Mr Judd afterwards. 'I never knew a piece of business settled so easily.'

The sequel was that other farmers wanted to sell their fields too. Mr Taylor and Mr Judd bought all they wanted for a fair amount. Jehovah Jireh!

Now, the buildings. How? Where would the money come from? Stones, brick and timber from a distance would cost a great deal. Locally little was obtainable. Or was it?

'Let's quarry our own stones,' Mr Taylor suggested. Although his degree was in medicine he decided to be his own architect. Employing men, they made their own bricks. Bricks were essential, of course, but what would happen when the time came to insert window frames, hang doors and roof the new building?

Just then a ship lay wrecked in Chefoo Bay. Sturdy oak . . . Norwegian pine . . . they purchased a large part of the wreck for rafters and heavy beams. Incredible that *that* ship should be named *The Christian*! A Shanghai newspaper carried an article which stated that *The Christian* had ceased going to sea, and had joined the CIM! Another wreck provided teak for the floors and its cabin fittings were just right for furnishings. The price was just right too — they could have as much as they liked for three shillings and ninepence per hundredweight.

Mr Judd wrote, 'I do not say that the house was well built, but it was wonderfully good, considering our lack of

experience.' Five rooms upstairs and five rooms down, with an outhouse and lean-to rooms as extras.'It was marvellously cheap,' he went on, 'and the Europeans in Chefoo were amazed at the rapidity with which it was put up. They could hardly believe their eyes when they saw it finished.'

And so Chefoo School stood — but as yet without pupils or teachers.

In actual fact Chefoo School's first headmaster was already in China. Mr Elliston too was sent to Chefoo's seaside for rest and recuperation, and was to stay for seven years. So 1881 brought together a building, Mr Judd's three sons and a qualified teacher. In a little room about twelve feet square the first lessons began.

News about CIM's venture in education travelled fast. Schooling for westerners was sparse in China, so applications began to pile in from all over the land and from all sorts of business people. The original plan for the school began to expand. Mr Taylor wrote in the mission magazine in August 1881,

'Among the various works we are proposing is that of a school for the children of missionaries and other foreign residents in China and we trust that through it the trial and expense of sending children home from China may in many cases be saved. Mr W.L. Elliston has already made a commencement and the number of pupils is about twelve with every prospect of increase.'

By the next April fourteen were on the roll and a new building was in course of erection. The following year more land was bought, which meant the boys could have their schooling separately. And so on those sunny slopes grew building after school building, as well as private houses. The once-silent shore was now a scene of delightful activity. Competent teachers who were full members of the mission cared for children from Kindergarten to College years.

By 1896 the dozen pupils had increased to over one hundred. *The Christian's* timber had served its purpose but now it was obvious that additional buildings were required. Again came the question marks. Money? Missionaries prayed. One day a letter came from a mission member saying, 'The Lord has laid it on my heart to bear the whole cost of building the school' — a school that would provide housing for a hundred boys and a separate building for eighty girls.

June 15th, 1896 was a memorable day. At four o'clock that afternoon the Foundation Stone was laid. Overhead the Union Jack, Stars and Stripes and Chinese flags waved together.

'Hitherto hath the Lord helped us.
  This foundation stone is laid
    To commemorate
  The faithfulness of God
    In connection with the
  China Inland Mission Schools
    which were founded A.D. 1881
  For the education of children of Missionaries
    The Lord will provide.
      June 15th 1896'

This song was written by Stanley Houghton and is sung frequently in Chefoo School today:

Jehovah Jireh

'THE LADS FOR WHOM HE DIED . . .'

Mr Norris was headmaster number two. He took over at Chefoo in 1886. Little did he know that his contribution to the school would be so brief.

With the help of Mr McCarthy, he got going with an enthusiasm which was to give the children the best possible education of their day.

'Since last June,' he wrote, 'we have received applications to take no fewer than 28 new pupils . . . From the plan (of the new school) you will see that a carpenter's shop is included in the building. This I desire to fit up with a turner's lathe, turning tools, and tools for wood-carving and fret-work.

'I hope to be able to send you soon a proposed curriculum of a six years' course for boys from nine to fifteen. From this you will see that, with the aid of Dr Douthwaite, I hope to make a study of natural science an important feature during the last two years of such a course. For this purpose scientific apparatus of all kinds will be needed, and I wish to begin at once to collect, as our fees are so small as to make my hopes of being able to expend for those things from the school income only faint ones. I should be glad to receive gifts of a microscope, telescope, magnetic batteries, chemical apparatus, apparatus to illustrate sound, light, and heat, diagrams to illustrate geology, botany, etc.

'Our library is slowly growing, and we have in it some

few more than two hundred volumes. I am anxious to cultivate in the boys, before they leave school, a taste for good literature.'

And so Mr Norris was full of plans. This time the Lord's plan was different.

One August evening in 1888, the boys were at work in their school room. China in August was *hot* . . . they had flung wide the doors and windows to catch any cool sea breeze wafting from the shore.

The evening lethargy was suddenly and viciously disturbed. All at once, the students heard the swift approach of an animal. A dog dashed into view . . . only a dog . . . but it kept rushing on, right into the classroom. Fiercely it snapped at the nearest boy, and he saw the foaming mouth.

'It's mad! Sir, a mad dog!' The boys, shouting in fear, climbed on their desks to escape the biting jaws.

Mr Norris jumped up in time to see the crazy animal tear off along the corridor. The dormitories! Small boys were down there getting ready for bed. Without a second thought, Mr Norris chased after the dog, knowing that those little boys were in grave danger. The Cranston family still remembers how one brother was shielded from it. Cornering the animal, the headmaster managed to divert it, but the angry beast flew at him, and got his fingers. Even then, Mr Norris made sure the creature was captured and killed before he left the building.

Perhaps he ought to let the doctor glance at the cut on his finger. It was little more than a scratch and seemed far from serious. The doctor cauterized it and both men forgot about it. Even when Mr Norris was taken ill three weeks later, it did not occur to folk at first to link his fever with the mad dog bite. Delirious, he grew rapidly worse. Could it possibly be hydrophobia? Soon there could be no doubt. about the work at Chefoo School. He had planned to do so much for the boys . . . he was so glad that Mr McCarthy could continue . . . the boys . . . Fred, Andrew, Donald, Henry, Foster, Sam . . .

And the boys didn't forget. For many years these verses hung on the white wall of their classroom in a simple black frame.

They bore him sadly to his early grave,
On that green slope that fronts the restless tide,
Their bright young faces awed to tearful calm —
    The lads for whom he died . . .
He loved them all and longed to make the boys
Brave, trusted, strong as English lads should be,
With gentle hearts and ready sympathies,
    Faithful, and bold and free.
Not dead! not dead! in the far years to come,
The lads he loved — their boyhood left behind,
Shall in his noble life — his early death,
    An inspiration find.
This seed-thought, planted sadly by his grave,
In future days its precious fruits shall bear,
Firing to acts of brave self-sacrifice
    The boys he held so dear.

WEI HAI WEI. ROAD. CHEFOO

YENTAI

Strangely, Chefoo was a misnomer! The port's name belonged to one era — the compartment of time when the white settlers enjoyed life there beside an arm of the great Pacific Ocean. Before those days, Chefoo was Yentai.

Yentai was once merely a small fishing village. Then war came. After the Anglo-French armies captured Peking, Yentai became a 'Treaty Port' — according to this treaty of 1858, certain towns were 'permitted to carry on trade with whomsoever they please and to proceed to and fro at pleasure with their merchandise.' Other privileges granted by the treaty included 'the right of residence, of buying or renting houses, of leaving land therein and of building churches, hospitals and cemeteries.'*

Heigh-ho then for the white businessmen, merchants, traders, sailors and . . . missionaries! By 1860 they were all there.

Not that Yentai or China were devoid of experience of foreigners before that. Forays right back into long-ago Chinese dynasties can discover Romans, Arabians, Tartars, Franciscans and Dominicans all interested in that land. As far back as 1600 there is evidence of Christian communities in Chefoo's Shantung province.

Why then did Yentai become Chefoo? Chefoo was actually just a small fishing village on the Bluff which was connected to the mainland by a sandspit; yet this was the name the foreigners adopted.

Now Yentai/Chefoo was open for foreign trade and its importance grew rapidly. In the one year 1875, just before the CIM schools came into existence, 707 vessels cleared from Chefoo port. Judging by the flags in the harbour, a mixed crowd must have been found on shore! By the time the school started, the population of Chefoo was 29,000 and growing.

23

Westerners revived the ancient craft of weaving pongee silk. An 1873 report mentioned the importance of the fruit trade, especially Shantung pears. It was Marco Polo who had described them glowingly as 'certain pears of enormous size, weighing as much as ten pounds a piece, the pulp of which is white and fragrant like a confection.' Or did he mean a coconut? Even a gold rush enlivens the records of that time, though hopes were disappointed.

But the reign of the whites barely lasted a century. The days were rich for those of 'The Settlement', and even more so for the western Chefusians who had acquired most of the East Beach. Then Communism came to China and it was goodbye to the settlers, goodbye to the strange white children who loved the beach.

* Article XI of the Treaty of Tientsin, 1858 (quoted from *Glimpses of the History of Chefoo*, by C.W. Schmidt, 1932)

SLOW TRAIN COMING

'What is a missionary?' asked a Sunday School teacher once.

'My dad's one,' a little voice piped up. 'He packs and unpacks his suitcase.'

Travel.

To plumb the depths of meaning in the word one hundred years ago in China, we need a map where the tiny scale is the only aid in forming a concept of the enormous distances. We need to have it register in our late twentieth-century minds that cars and even trains are modern innovations; that 'par avion' was unheard of; that mules on muddy tracks and boats poled along sluggish, mustard-coloured waters were accepted as the norm by the missionary mind.

Then too, twentieth-century rationalism accepts the fact but doesn't really comprehend that China is *vast*. The Overseas Missionary Fellowship of today was then the China *Inland* Mission. 'Inland' for Marjory meant she was among those who never went home again once they arrived at Chefoo. She and her sisters lived there, year in, year out, from 1904-1911. Once during that period they had a long summer visit from their parents. The long khaki ribbon of the Yangtse Kiang made the union possible — the Yangtse which serpentines its way through central China for 3,100 miles, the fifth longest waterway in the world.

'And yet,' Marjory summarizes, 'we look back on it all lovingly — the place to which *God* sent us — the place we loved — the link between us and hundreds who were there as children . . .'

Arthur's memories stretch right back to the beginning of the century, too. How primitive his home conditions were and how difficult the travel! It took Arthur's dad thirteen

CHINA

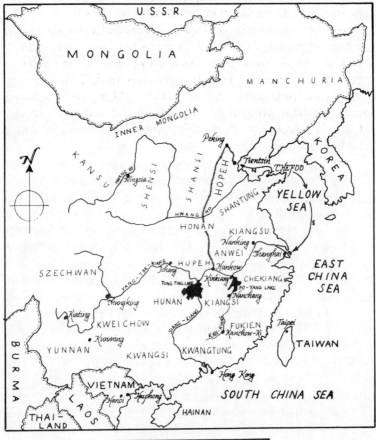

Scale:- km
1 : 20 000 000
200   0   200   400   500

International Boundaries :

Railway lines :

Steamer Routes :

days to get him to the Yangtse in 1906 — on the first lap of his journey to Chefoo! No railroads then — he travelled in a *hua-kan* or mountain chair, and it was a junk, not a steam boat, which negotiated the interminable river.

South Kiangsi was a mere 300 miles from Chefoo so Margaret was one of those who had the tremendous thrill of going home for Christmas. Of course, more time was spent on the journey than at home. Usually those whose home was accessible for holidays spent three weeks getting there, a fortnight at home and three weeks making it back!

Margaret's normal route home involved the steamer trip south to Shanghai under the escort of teachers. From there a parent took over the dwindling party as various destinations along the Yangtse were reached. Thirty miles, a train journey and one day later Margaret reached Nanchang, the provincial capital — the only Chefusian left. Expressively she drew this incredible word picture of the rest of the journey.

'My mother met me in Nanchang, in a Chinese sailing boat on which she had come down the Kan River, a tributary of the Yangtse. This journey had once, legend says, been done in ten days, though that may well have been an apocryphal story. It *could* take three weeks depending on the wind. With a north wind, the boatmen had a relative holiday and we whizzed along, both sails spread, doing, I once remember, 50 miles in one day! But that was only once. When the wind failed us, the boatmen either walked along the edge of the boat poling it along or else walked on the bank pulling it just as their ancestors had done for thousands of years. At that point there was nothing to prevent me walking on the shore also. I even remember once having a swim!'

How did they occupy the time? One lovely aspect of the long river trip was the way mother and daughter, little by little, began to know each other again. How precious that was after the sharp sting of ten months' separation.

And then they accomplished so much! Mother was always accompanied by her sewing machine and her baby organ. To the entertainment of the crew Margaret had to practise every day on the organ. She couldn't help it that she was tone deaf and derived little from the exercises. With the sewing machine, they reviewed, planned and made her clothes for the coming year. Even Mrs Gaskell's *Cranford* and Thackeray's *Vanity Fair* are recalled when thoughts go back to sail boats on the Kan River.

But the real excitement came in the last few days. Father would then be on holiday too, sailing downstream and approaching *their* boat in *his*. As the possible but unsure meeting place came nearer the boatmen would shout to each other, 'Any foreign devil aboard?' And then when the answer was 'Yes', it happened. Father transferred from his boat to theirs for the remaining sixty miles or so. At least they had his company for the rather dangerous rapid shooting.

But the 'old' days were nearing their end, and innovations were reaching even Inland China. A long railway came to be built through China's central plain. Then the

Boat on the rapids, 1915

party would start out in a large carriage with all their luggage. 'All' meant trunks, bedrolls — even food, to be supplemented at the stations en route. The carriage boasted a passage right down the middle, on either side of which were rows of plain hard wooden seats. A trunk might be several inches lower or higher than the benches but no matter, it went well enough between them as a support for stretched-out bedding rolls and sleeping children.

'One adventure will always remain in my mind', Margaret concludes. 'I don't expect anyone to believe this happened, but it did. With many other witnesses I was there when it happened. Early one evening a girl fell off the train!'

In the dark, as the train was (mercifully) chugging slowly alongside works on the line, one Chefusian visited the rather primitive toilet facilities, exposed to the elements, in between carriages. On her return did she mistake the lanterns on the line for the carriage lights? However she came to do it, she stepped right off the train and fell to the railway line below, to be helped to her feet by a Chinese workman. Immediately she was missed, the escort had the train stopped. He and a couple of the boys walked back and found her, none the worse for such an extraordinary mishap!

*   *   *

Beau's was a less time-consuming journey. His terminus was Hankow — actually on the River Yangtse. The journey involved the two-day boat trip to Shanghai and then four days by steamer up the river. But even that shorter trip, in later days, was fraught with difficulties for Beau's time at Chefoo coincided almost exactly with the Sino-Japanese war. He missed the entire third form year since, having gone home for the holidays, he was trapped up the Yangtse because the Japanese had occupied Shanghai.

Several Chefusians were making for the South West — right into Yunnan. They belonged to the Hong Kong group which was an offshoot from the Shanghai party. This tale illustrates so beautifully God's loving care on a very difficult journey. His provision for the little group and the answers to prayers they experienced in their trials reflect the light of His concern as a precious stone glints amidst the gravel in a pan.

'I wish I could tell you more of our trips home for Christmas', this story-teller narrates. 'At the end of November there was a buzz of excitement as the playroom was all laid out with boxes and cases.' Early December saw the chartered ships setting out. 'The Shanghai party, 170 of us, was the biggest. Not much fun in the three-to-four-day run to Shanghai. Then we were all divided up. What a headache it must have been for the mission home at Sinza Road!'

That year 25 went on towards Hong Kong where they arrived four days later with Miss Kemp, who had been co-opted to escort them, little realizing the testings ahead for those fifteen who had still further to go.

Transhipping at Haiphong, they discovered the visa only Hanoi could provide was lacking. That afternoon in desperation all fifteen caught the last train to Hanoi. Then started a crawl from hotel to hotel.

'Sorry. No room.'

At last the only hotel left to challenge was the grandest in town!

'We sat on our cases and prayed,' she continues. 'Miss Kemp went in . . .

'"Sorry, no room . . ."

'But it so happened that at that moment, a lady and a gentleman who had been on our ship came to the desk and heard our plight. The gentleman gave up his room to us. Four of us big girls slept in a double bed! Miss Kemp had the single bed. Catherine and Kathryn, two little prep school girls, shared their bed with the French lady who had been so attracted by them on board ship. And the boys slept in the lounge. The gentleman who gave up his room was a personal adviser to Chiang Kai Shek.'

Next morning, even though the bill was cut in two, a wire to CIM for more money was despatched immediately!

How relieved Miss Kemp must have been when the hotel found an empty annexe for them after that. Yet the tedious journey had lengthened by several days. For the story-teller, three more days of train travel and two extra nights in Chinese hotels lay ahead. That second day she counted 165 tunnels. On the third day, dusk fell at last. Some parents loomed out of the darkness on the station platform . . . 'Alas,' she remembers, 'not mine. Daddy still wasn't fully recovered from typhoid fever — so I had to travel another three days by horse and mountain chair escorted by friends till Mummy and Daddy met me.'

At long last mother, father and daughter were together. Home. Taku nestled in the hills of Yunnan but after enjoying it for two precious weeks only, she had to begin the whole journey again in reverse.

Is it any wonder that one contributor to these stories comments — 'Those were the days when to be a missionary meant something . . .'?

John was from the same lonely region — Yunnan — but because his schooldays were earlier in the century he was less fortunate. 'My father and I journeyed 2,500 miles to take me to school at the age of six . . . From that time on I spent exactly one month "under the same roof" as my parents and family. Because it was impossible for *me* to go home for the holidays, I was one of the "left behinds" every year of my childhood . . .'

*   *   *

And what of the trip northwards? A quick look at the map will show that the port of Chefoo lies between Tientsin to the north and Shanghai to the south. These two larger ports ended the first lap of the journey for the two Chefoo sailing parties. Messrs Butterfield and Swire were responsible for conveying the northern party to Tientsin; five days later the boat returned to take the southern party to Shanghai.

Stanley belonged to the northern party — his parents were located in central Honan Province. In the 1920s the only forms of travel from Chefoo were ship, train or mule cart. The bitter winter weather saw to it that the shivering little group was clad in overcoats, balaclava helmets and gloves. More often than not, they found the sea rough on the passage to Tientsin. Was it ever a relief to see the muddy water of the Taku River emptying itself into the sea!

From Tientsin a reserved train carriage took the children inland. Those going further still would take to the 'carts' — always the most exciting means of transport! Considering the atrociously muddy roads, the bogs in which they frequently stuck, the snow, the presence of a small military escort to keep bandits at bay — well, considering all this, they did quite well if they managed thirty miles per day!

But even the steamer trip wasn't always straightforward, as this sea saga describes:

'Spirits were high as the party bound for Tientsin set off for their annual holiday. But the ship's captain was apprehensive as we rounded the Bluff, that familiar promontory with an island at its tip right across from the school. The glass was falling fast and though the sea was calm there was an unnatural stillness in the atmosphere; his experience of coastal navigation warned him of a storm. Before long it broke upon us, the wind screaming in the rigging and lashing the spray against the ship. Order was given for all to vacate the deck lounge and go below to the cabins. The seamen tied stout ropes to form a kind of rail from the saloon to the hatch stairs. Strong hands grasped each in turn and children were passed from hand to hand across this hazardous stretch of deck where a hundred-mile-an-hour gale threatened to sweep away any obstacles in its path.

'We were told to lie in our bunks, but this was no simple matter as the ship rolled and plunged crazily in the boiling seas, and all we could do was to hold on to whatever we could and hope for the best. One of the cheerful cabin boys appeared at our door, and giving the thumbs down sign said "Ship soon down bottomside", and some of us felt we could almost wish it were true. Most of us were desperately sick, and we heard later that some of the seasoned officers on board suffered this indignity, but even so jokes were bandied from cabin to cabin and we endeavoured to laugh it off.

'There was nothing below deck to mark the passage of time, and no real schedule, though the steward was busy slipping and sloshing his way round with biscuits, bread

HERE IS CHEFOO

Far from our homes in wild Yunnan,
  In Szechuan or in Hu,
From brigand-fested old Honan,
  And far off Kansuh, too,
Across the wide plain of Sian
  We flock into Chefoo!

We travel all the ways we can
  except perhaps canoe.
Raft, litter, cart, or luggage van,
  Most anything will do.
Train, motor, steamer and sampan
  All help to reach Chefoo.

Our lives here, quite a lengthy span,
  Are limited in view.
To us it's more important than
  London and New York too!
Really, we don't see how you can
  Be asking, "Where's Chefoo?"

Though small upon the map, you scan
  The spot that marks Chefoo,
Within the heart of many a man
  And many a woman too,
It's larger in proportion than
  A Continent or two.

And when we reach life's rubicon
  And take a backward view,
There'll be few memories that can
  Outshine those of Chefoo!

A Chefoo Resident
(from CSA magazine, December 1961)

and oranges. News filtered through that we were lying up in the lee of an island, and all anchors were out as we endeavoured to ride out the storm. Boards creaked, anchors dragged and chains strained. Spray froze as it struck the ship, leaving a thick coat of ice on the windward side and giving us a decided list to starboard, which in itself was another hazard. The first mate was imprisoned in his ice-locked cabin and when eventually the storm subsided he had to be chiselled out.

'The typhoon blew itself out and the seemingly endless battering and buffeting, rolling and pitching, gradually subsided. At last we heard the pleasant chug of the ship's engines as we churned a course through the turbulent sea towards Tientsin. Provisions were strictly rationed, as the voyage which normally lasts 48 hours had now taken four days. There was a wonderful *esprit de corps* as games, charades and impromptu concerts were organized in which even the captain joined, while Mr Arthur Taylor, master in charge of the party, quipped and joked in his inimitable way, to the accompaniment of uproarious laughter. We were quite prepared to sing a lusty "He's a jolly good fellow" to captain, officers and all the humorous heroes of this episode, but in our hearts we knew that, just as God had prepared a means of salvation for Jonah, so for us he had prepared an island just in the right place to be a shelter from the storm.

'No news had got through to anxious parents waiting in Tientsin until the ship had reached the bar at Taku and the pilot took over navigation up the small river to the city dock. The CIM doxology was sung as families were reunited, and I suppose no one was more relieved than the master in charge. Certainly in his 25 years as mission representative in Scotland he must have told and retold the story a hundred times, a story of God's unfailing love, care, protection and provision.'

Sad incidents and loneliness, holiday fun and excitement, family reunions and sorrowful farewells all come under the umbrella of God's care, of His all-wise, sovereign overruling — for purposes of His own beyond the reasonings of our finite minds.

One group, ready to leave the Chefoo School in Kuling, had their booking on a river boat for two days ahead. That exciting piece of holiday information had already been announced. It was rather a shock, therefore, when acting headmaster Mr Martin made a second statement that evening.

'I've received strong guidance,' he began, 'that we should not travel on that boat.'

Sighs of disappointment greeted his comment.

'We'll try to get a booking on the next,' he continued.

Everyone knew it would mean a week's delay, more red tape . . . The atmosphere in the hall breathed anticlimax.

Three days later at evening prayers, news reached the hushed group that the boat they would have travelled on had been torpedoed and sunk, with no lives saved . . .

They caught another river steamer two days later.

*　　*　　*

Mr Sparks was a non-swimmer. Perhaps that is why he was apprehensive about meeting the steamers when they arrived in Chefoo Harbour. In a small sampan he ferried the children from the ship to the shore.

The quiet confidence of his little charges challenged his nervousness. 'Why are you afraid of the waves? God is looking after us,' one little girl assured him.

Tragically he was drowned on a subsequent duty call. A launch suddenly appeared from behind a steamer, ramming and upsetting the little sampan in which he was travelling.

However, one can't help noticing that though travel in China was then so potentially dangerous, again and again the Chefoo children arrived wihout mishap.

In the early years of the century, the beautiful mountain resort of Kuling had also been the location of a little prep school. One winter Contie set off for school. To be only six and travelling in a mountain chair with just little Bertie for company was quite an adventure. Already the escorting teacher, with her other little charges, was out of sight. No one had caught up with them from behind either, after the long haul across the plains.

Snow started to sprinkle the mountain tops.

Was it too risky for the coolies to carry the two little ones up the steep slope — a narrow path, hugging the mountain side precariously, curving ever upwards to Kuling seven miles away? The bearers stopped, set the children down, found shelter and began to refresh themselves with tea and probably rice wine. In the gathering storm the pathway was deserted. A numbing sense of vulnerability, like the grey mountain mist, descended on the two lonely figures. Bertie began to wail loudly.

But what was that? Steadily, reassuringly footsteps crunched towards them in the snow. It just 'happened' that Mr Judd chose *that* day to walk down from Kuling where he had been supervising building operations. In the fairy-tale world of snowflakes and seeming emptiness, he heard Bertie's howling. In his protection they found the CIM home in Kui Kiang six miles back. Seeing the snow creeping down the mountains, the other thirty children hadn't started the climb. Trials were soon forgotten in a merry game of 'Blind Man's Buff' with their companions.

A day or two later, it was safe to start off afresh. This time no hitches cropped up. Almost seventy years later Contie still remembers 'the breathless beauty of the snow-clad pine trees, in a completely silent world — except for the faint tinkle of music from trickling streams steeply falling into little pools, as we climbed ever higher, our chairs swaying on the shoulders of the sturdy, sure-footed bearers.

'And there was Mr Lindsay outside the school gate, with a sledge for the youngest, while *we* walked along the valley road to stretch our legs and warm up.'

*　　*　　*

Today travel is still a hurdle for Chefusians. Perhaps the greatest distances now involve journeys from the circumference of North Thailand, Java and Taiwan to the beautiful central hub — Chefoo School's little green valley in the Cameron Highlands, Peninsular Malaysia.

Just a few years ago the teacher in charge of a travel party fought down a sense of panic as her fingers dialled the Chefoo number from far away on the borders of Thailand.

'Hello? It's Molly here. Yes, I know I should be on the train to Thailand, but . . .'

There on the border from Malaysia into Thailand, the immigration officials discovered that two little boys, aged nine and six, did not have the correct stamp in their visas. The officers put the boys off the train — the train that had been chugging for several hours now towards Mum and Dad at home. There was nothing else for it but that the leader of the party should disembark too. In the loneliness of the foreign border town, in torrential rain, she stood with her two little charges watching the train, with all their companions on board, hiss out of the station.

It was 11.30 am. Already they'd been travelling around the clock. Midnight had seen them leave the stillness of the jungled darkness at Chefoo. All night they travelled in taxis down the winding mountain road and had sped northwards across the lowlands towards Thailand. By 7 am they'd reached the station. Now, well on their way to Bangkok, this bombshell had exploded. Brydon and Michael were to be allowed no further. Even finding a taxi back presented problems. It was a long time before they were back on the Malaysian highway, speeding towards the Immigration office in Kuala Lumpur.

Day wore on as the weary miles flew by. A glorious sunset streaked the sky to the west. The two little boys had fallen asleep so Molly was alone with her thoughts. Why was she here? What was she doing hurtling towards Kuala Lumpur in the darkness and balminess of a tropical night? This was a land she'd only vaguely known about two years previously. The story went back a long way — right to the time when Molly herself had been a little girl and had asked the Lord Jesus to be her Saviour. It was true that He changed lives. He'd changed hers to the extent that she wanted to serve Him — *any*where. And He had chosen Chefoo School, Malaysia.

When had she last been able to get her head down? Exhaustion threatened to overwhelm her. As they passed the road that led to the mountains and to school she wondered if she could keep going without sleep, but as another midnight approached, so did Kuala Lumpur.

Mission guest homes! What a joy they have been throughout the century. Here was another in a new land, different welcoming arms, different helpers but the same precious Lord's love — reaching out to two little ones and an overtired escort.

Two days later, the weariness forgotten, a fully-rested trio found themselves in Bangkok, after a short flight with passports correct in every detail.

The train journey they should have been on was beset with further complications — amusing in retrospect but causing problems at the time.

Little seven-year-old Rachel was to disembark in the middle of the night at a small station, six hours from Bangkok. After rousing Rachel from her sleeper and sorting out her baggage and huge teddy, one of the remaining escorts hustled the little girl on to the platform before even the grey dawn of morning appeared in the Thai sky. Peering through the gloom, he searched for Mum and Dad. Were those two shapes at the far end of the platform . . .? Another adult hurriedly jumped off the train to stand by Rachel while he went to investigate.

That was when the train driver decided to pull out of the station — leaving three instead of one on the platform!

Fortunately the one escort left, feeling like the last green bottle hanging on the wall, was a loving capable Mum who bravely landed her charges in Bangkok just as the new day's tropical heat began to flood the city.

Little Rachel* won't travel with the Chefoo children any more. She is in heaven now, with her entire family — due to a tragic accident that very holiday.

But perhaps the journey's frustrations would have seemed of less moment had the Bangkok party of Christmas 1977 realized that theirs was the last mammoth train journey the Chefoo children would need to undergo.

Before the next holidays, Overseas Missionary Fellowship was able to grant the money required to fly the children home to Thailand — just like their friends who lived across a sea in Taiwan or Indonesia.

Rachel as a Japanese lady

---

* Rachel Gordon-Smith, who died with eleven others in January 1978, at Manorom, Thailand.

'Thank You, Heavenly Father, for those who have made this possible by giving so generously in the homelands . . . enough for even the smallest child to be catered for in travel to and from Chefoo School.'

Today, travel arrangements, which have really been quite a headache throughout the century, mean planning to ferry the children to various airports. From there, the main part of their journey is undertaken in a short comfortable flight. Only those living comparatively near the school forfeit the delight of a plane trip!

On the way home to Thailand

'OF SHOES AND SHIPS AND SEALING WAX' . . . and oranges?

China Inland Mission,
1531 Sinza Road,
Shangai.
February 1, 1935
6.30 p.m.

Dear Friend,

We deeply regret to have to report that Butterfield and Swire's *S.S. Tungchow*, by which the party of children sailed for Chefoo on the 29th January at 10.45 a.m., has not yet arrived there, and though the vessel is installed with wireless apparatus, no reply to the messages which have been sent has been received. As it has been learned that the seas have been calm and the atmosphere clear since the seamen sailed from this port, the Shipping Company fear that the vessel has been pirated. The British Naval Authorities have sent out a cruiser, a sloop and a destroyer, one of which carries aircraft, to search the whole of the China coast. Butterfield and Swire have also sent out steamers to endeavour to locate the *Tungchow*.

We desire to express to you our heartfelt sympathy in the anxiety which this news will occasion you. This anxiety is shared by us, and we at this centre are meeting this evening for united intercession.

With kindest regards,
Believe me,
Yours very sincerely,
G.W. Gibb
(General Director)

No one had paid the slightest attention when 24 Chinese 'passengers' in flowing gowns had boarded the *Tungchow*. They looked ordinary enough. In fact everything had seemed quite normal on that glorious January day as the 74 Chefoo children and five staff members embarked at Shanghai. Tears had found a course down some small cheeks but soon the ship-load of children was reminiscing about Christmas and showing off their new toys.

Supper time ticked round. The little prep school children marched towards the saloon with their teachers, not knowing that the billowing Chinese garb of the pseudo-passengers was being exchanged below deck for sinister pirate gear, nor that the crew and travellers were in jeopardy as surely as the dusk was darkening to night.

Thud! Crack! The noisy Christmassy chatter around the table came to an instant fullstop as sudden sounds on deck shattered the evening harmony. Yes, there it was again — smack, bang, pistol shots, shouts, scurrying of feet, scuffle and — death. The *Tungchow* was in the hands of a pirate gang.

The saloon changed roles and became the setting for a horror movie. Doors were flung open as the various compartments of the ship ejected their crew members, officers, children, teachers and the captain into the packed dining area.

Terrified, the children saw pistols pointing across the room. They crowded to the back, their hands up like victims in a terrorist raid — which, in fact, they were. The captain, his hands also held high and despite the danger facing him of a quick-firing gun, tried to calm the children. 'The pirates aren't here to get *you*,' he soothed. 'They'll not harm you. You wait and see. Everything will be all right.'

His brave words did not still the apprehension of the escorts. The situation was grave. Any gun could go off any moment, even by accident. Mr Duncan was being searched, and handed over his dollar notes, but the gangsters were really trying to satisfy themselves about firearms in case of any retaliation. They demanded that all firearms on the ship were to be delivered up, and only then could hands be lowered and permission given to continue with supper.

But nobody felt like eating — staff supervising with pistols against their backs, the ship rolling at the mouth of the Yangtse, the saloon airless and little ones with tears still streaming down their cheeks. What did they want, these villains? It wasn't a surprise to hear that all money must be handed in. It amounted to little but, to the children, the loss of their Christmas present money was a big thing. It wasn't only control of the *Tungchow* they wanted, was it? They had that now, completely. The captain was goaded back to the bridge guarded by four gunmen, the children sent back to their cabins. The *Tungchow's* course was turned towards the south to the pirates' headquarters in Bias Bay. The ship was disguised by painting two white rings around the funnel and brushing out its name. Now in spite of the trouble they were in, they appeared to the outside world to be merely a Japanese cargo boat.

'We're heading south for the pirates' base where we will be prisoners for life,' John moaned to Cliff in a small fear-filled voice.

'They'll line us up and shoot us when we reach land,' speculated Duncan.

One Russian guard was dead already, shot as he tried to fight off the gang when they had advanced over the deck initially. His body was ignobly turfed over the side of the *Tungchow*.

The situation was critical. The boys looked to the staff. This God they served, could He rescue them? They'd been taught that He was an 'ever-present help in time of trouble'. But did the teachers really believe that — now that the crunch had come? Did they have the peace *now* that God had promised to His followers?

The dilemma darkened. The pirates had paid four thousand dollars for information that the *Tungchow* was carrying a cargo of silver dollars. Now they found out that the tip-off had been erroneous. The *Tungchow's* cargo was much more precious than mere dollars with so many special lives on board — but not in the eyes of the pirates. All they found was a quantity of unsigned dollar notes which were useless. Surely all hell would be let loose . . .

Yet a strange thing happened. On the second day of

captivity the pirates were — friendly! Yes, friendly — even joking with the senior boys and rolling cratefuls of plundered oranges to the smaller children.

The secret of this remarkable and unlikely turn of events lay where the real battle was being waged in the heavenlies. At CIM Headquarters in Shanghai the mission members would be meeting — as they always had done in every crisis in its seventy-year-old history — for prayer to their all-sovereign Lord.

And could it have been merely coincidence that on the very morning of the voyage God had assured them, through the *Daily Light* reading, 'Thou compassest my path and my lying down'? Mrs Hoste, widow of the previous General Director, had sent a little note to one staff member saying, 'My Presence shall go with thee and I will give thee rest'. This was just what they needed to know. She had added, 'Let not your heart be troubled, neither let it be afraid.' How could she have realized in advance that they would need to hang their very lives on these promises during the voyage?

Then there was that other prayer meeting — the time when they'd been due to leave yet Mr Duncan had felt unsettled about the *Tungchow* because conditions were cramped for the seventy-plus in his party.

'Let's ask God about it,' suggested one of the executives at Headquarters.

It was *after* prayer that they unanimously decided to go ahead. After all 'it would only be for two nights'.

That's how it was that Miss Priestman could read to her boys on the last day of January, 'What shall we say to these things? If God be for us, who can be against us?' and the boys sensed her peace.

'We tremble to think what might have been,' Beth wrote over forty years later. 'But God . . .'

The *Tungchow* was sailing in new waters towards the pirates' headquarters, without an up-to-date chart. The ship had not taken that course for years yet Captain James Gordon Smart calmly steered his precious cargo along the dangerous coastline.

One threat which had chilled their hearts was the chief

pirate's warning, 'Any incidents on the voyage and the children will all be shot.' On the third day the pirates decided to make their getaway and it was imperative for everyone's safety that no one should hinder them or try to rescue the *Tungchow* at that point.

The children below deck could hear gunfire, shots and shouting as the gang tried to commandeer a junk to get to land. The third attempt was successful. All seemed to be going according to their plans. But as the boat returned from the nearby island for the remainder of the loot — silk, cloth and supplies of food — a plane from *H.M.S. Hermes* swooped overhead. Twenty pirates, now dressed as wealthy tycoons, were waiting on deck to be taken ashore. What would happen now after such a dire threat? The safety of the children was once again in the balance.

The twenty false businessmen were transformed to a panic-stricken horde. Hurriedly they ordered the crew to lower a boat. They grabbed the chief engineer, the wireless operator and four Chinese members of the crew. With them as hostages they clambered down a rope and put off.

The plane flew low again. Did God prompt an officer to chalk in large letters on deck, 'Don't fire on small boat'?

'Look! Pirates are leaving!' Below deck a teacher's voice was suspended in her reading as one boy near the port-hole called out the news of what was happening above. Like a broken snare, the cabin discharged its small occupants to enjoy all that was going on as the drama came to a conclusion.

They saw the pirates beach on the island and shoot holes in the *Tungchow's* small boat to prevent the escape of the hostages. Yet they were free — for the pirates scattered into hiding. The wireless operator made for a nearby hill and signalled for help. Soon another small boat was setting out from the parent ship to bring them back.

The rescue plane again dived low from the sky. At last the pilot seemed convinced that he hadn't found a Japanese boat unloading cargo, but that it was indeed the *Tungchow*, which every British ship on the China coast was looking out for.

It was Friday afternoon. The tension had wonderfully

and suddenly snapped. 'Here, look!' shouted one of the boys, the new freedom making his voice shrill with excitement, 'A pullover! It's his — the chief pirate's! Wow, what a find!' This sent them all scurrying to search for more souvenirs to prove that *they* had been on a pirated ship — the one the whole world, by now, was anxious about.

So the end of the afternoon saw them heading for Hong Kong, escorted by *H.M.S. Dainty*. Police launches put out to meet them. The second engineer, who had been seriously injured in the attack, was rushed ashore first in a launch, and an ambulance was awaiting him on the wharf.

It was supper time but no one was interested in food. Everyone wanted to be on deck, to be really part of this afterpiece. Yet bed-time came round and it was a must to climb into their bunks once more. And while the children were asleep the *S.S. Tungchow* anchored in Hong Kong harbour.

Dawn brought the press. Reporters urgently transferred the children's impressions to paper,

'I saw a man shot . . .'

'I was scared the first night the pirates took the boat.'

'I heard a bang and watched a little red ring come on his shirt.'

'We were afraid they would kill us if the British Navy were to come.'

But Mr J.N. Duncan, who was heading up the Chefoo party, gave the official account which was flashed to America and Britain.

'The pirates seized the vessel at 6 p.m. on Tuesday, and for three days looted it to their hearts' content while they steered for Bias Bay.

'The Russians fought for a little while, but the pirates outnumbered the guards, and soon subdued them. The pirates didn't molest the children, but the youngsters were very frightened for the three days.

'Yesterday planes from the *Hermes* flew over the vessel, and the pirates hurried ashore with the loot, taking some hostages who were subsequently released. After this the ship headed for Hong Kong, and was soon picked up by a British destroyer.

'The children were kept in a saloon for three days by a young pirate leader, who showed them some consideration. The children took the matter well and without panic — in fact, I'd say pluckily.'

The reception of the Chefusians in Hong Kong and Shanghai and, later, at Chefoo made most of the young ones forget the trauma of the previous days and feel that the whole adventure had been worth it! What publicity! What a welcome! They were famous — all over the world!

The suspense was over too for the parents. They lined Shanghai's quayside as the ship drew up to the wharf. And then — yes, they broke into praise to that almighty God for whom they worked on those shores. *He*'d led them there. For Him, their children had gone to boarding school. It was for Him they'd been travelling in a group without their parents; for Him they were exposed to danger. And He knew that. He'd sent His angels to protect His own.

> 'O God, our help in ages past,
>   Our hope for years to come,
> Our shelter from the stormy blast,
>   And our eternal home.
>
> Under the shadow of thy throne
>   Thy saints have dwelt secure;
> Sufficient is Thine arm alone,
>   And our defence is sure.'

* * *

One day, during the seventies, a visitor came to Chefoo, Malaysia. She loved the mission; she loved the school. Rather than touring the beautiful premises that morning or sight-seeing on the trails of the jungled mountains, she borrowed a teacher's bed-sit and spent the hours in prayer.

'I felt burdened for the children,' she explained afterwards, 'and God has reassured me. He has given me a vision of His care for them. I saw an angel, strong and powerful, like a mighty warrior, hovering over this little green valley, His flaming sword turning in all directions.' Didn't Elisha's servant have his eyes opened one day, too, to see God's forces protecting the Israelites?

The Lord Jesus Himself said, 'See that you do not despise one of these little one; for I tell you that in heaven their angels always behold the face of my Father who is in heaven.'*

'Thank you, Heavenly Father, for the wonderful part Your angels play in the safety of our Chefoo children. You have answered the prayers of many, world-wide, and have given them Your Protection in hundreds of vulnerable journeys.'

* Matthew 18.10

DRIFTWOOD

'Dead man found on beach.'
Who discovered him? Was he Chinese? Was he washed in
from the ocean? The old diary doesn't say. It merely adds
mercifully that he was covered with a mat. The reaction of
Chefoo schoolboys would have been worth recording but
the cryptic entry stands on its own like a clue to a seaside
mystery story.

Yet it wasn't fiction. Things happened by the sea, and
Chefoo School experienced a dimension of living that only
the coastline could give. A richness invaded their lives,
summer and winter, because of that inlet of the beautiful
Pacific on their doorstep. Each student remembers the
golden days. 'My heart warms,' wrote one, 'as I think of
that lovely place nestling between the hills and the sea. The
ocean at Chefoo became part of our living.'

The shore was ever there — inviting picnics, boating,
swimming, fun on the winter's ice, exploration. It even
offered a few macabre incidents to spice life, like the
discovery of a pole from which two cages hung. Closer
inspection revealed human skulls! Headmaster Pa Bruce
knew what to do that day . . . the second beach was
suddenly 'off limits'!

That beach wasn't always out of bounds, though. 'Such
happy memories!' they recall, 'particularly a breakfast
picnic at Second Beach when we ate grapes and corn bread
while sitting on the rocks with our feet dangling in the
water. Bliss!'

It would be difficult to say which aspect of seashore life
was most enjoyed. After sixty years, one Chefusian thinks,
'I was most interested in swimming. Chefoo being on a bay,
there was no undertow, and how we did love diving
through the billows. Every summer a two-mile swim from

one promontory to the other was held and when I was twelve I accomplished this in the company of my dad. Our family bathing house was not far from that of the Boys' School and we used to watch them burst out of the shed and scamper down the beach — all arms and legs! Mother called them "The Spiders"!'

One girl who went to Chefoo in 1904 recalls that the boys could swim three miles but the girls were only to attempt one. 'We were the weaker sex!' she explained with an exclamation mark and that solved all the inequality problems of that year! In the summer every day except Sunday was a swimming day.

Even though the beach did skirt the school it wasn't taken for granted. The waves were mastered only through a resolute spirit of daring on the part of both pupils and staff. The splash of bravado came about like this:—

'The method of teaching the art of swimming was rather Victorian,' recalls Stan, 'in keeping with the times, and, while rough, ready and primitive (for the boys, at least) it served its purpose and made us hardy, fearless and almost tireless swimmers . . . About ten of the younger boys would be taken out in a boat, in charge of the swimming master, a tough, red-headed, rawboned Scotsman. Older boys would be swimming casually around the boat, to prevent accidents. When all was ready, the instructor would ask the first shivering and apprehensive lad: "Do you want to jump in, dive in, or be thrown in?" Usually the victim would say hesitantly, "I guess I'll jump in, sir." "Then jump!" said the instructor . . . Down into the depths would go the boy, the water becoming murkier as he went . . . He would take a mouthful or two of salt water, and then, just as he thought his last hour had come, he would rise to the surface, spluttering and half-drowned . . . A senior boy would grab him by the hair, and tow him to the boat, where he would be hauled up unceremoniously, like a sack of wet fish. There he would sit on the edge of the long boat, coughing the water out of his lungs, eyes streaming, and watching the efforts of his fellow victims . . .

'A few minutes later the first boy's turn would come around again. "Do you want to jump in, dive in, or be

thrown in?" the master would ask. "Guess I'll jump in, sir,"
would be the probable reply. "OK, Smith, Jones or Robin-
son" (or whatever the boy's name was), the instructor
would say. "Remember you are not a fish! This time keep
your mouth shut and hold your nose. You cannot stay
under long because the body is lighter than water. When
you reach the surface, simply kick with your feet, and
paddle with your hands and arms until you reach the boat
— just like a dog." Following these simple instructions the
boy usually made the boat the second time . . . And thus his
swimming career would begin. Improvement came gradually with practice, and by watching the older boys. The
following summer the beginner of yesteryear would in all
likelihood be able to swim a quarter mile, then a half mile,
then one, two or three miles. As I intimated above, it was
rather a shattering experience. However, the fact remained
that the system achieved the desired results. It produced
good, easy, confident swimmers!'

Summer in Chefoo was the more golden because of the
'long stretches of shimmering sandy beaches with occasion-

al cliffs and rocky points. During those halcyon days we played cricket and tennis, roamed the hills and beaches and countryside or, favourite of all, swam and cavorted like sea-otters and dolphins in the blue waters of the Yellow Sea. Most of the boys and many of the girls could swim anything from one to three miles easily by the time they graduated or left Chefoo. Altogether it was a near-perfect atmosphere in which to bring up children.'

The beginning of the century saw a group of boys at Chefoo who still laugh when they remember the trick they played on Mr Alty! As duty master for a group of bathing Chefusians, Judy, as he was unceremoniously called, was sculling around one day in a dinghy. Approaching the raft, he challenged Arthur to dive under his boat and come up on the other side. Just at that stage of term, the class had been studying Shakespeare's *Julius Caesar*. Unbidden, a couplet darted into Arthur's mind:

'Caesar said to me, "Darest thou Cassius now
Plunge into the Tiber and come up on the other side?'
Arthur dived.

The dinghy carrying an unsuspecting Mr Alty was momentarily above him. Reaching high, Arthur pushed out the plug.

Judy looked hard over the side of the boat, watching for an emerging Arthur. And Arthur surfaced. Joining his classmates on the raft, he parodied,

'Twas on a bright and sunny day,
Judy said to me, "Darest thou Parry now
Plunge under this boat of mine and come up t'other
side?"

Upon the word,' he added, 'accoutred as I was, I plunged in and bade him look out!' To the merriment of the dripping crew on the raft, Judy was seen pulling for the shore as the boat rapidly filled with water!

Sometimes the frolicking gave rise to strange consequences. During a storm early one September, two boys made their way through the surf below the *bund* and climbed up onto the causeway opposite the North Gate of the Strand Hotel. At that time, in the thirties, the Japanese had taken command of the whole hotel with its many bungalows. It

Note on the 'Chefoo Schools Association' crest:

The emblem may be described as a Chinese dolphin — referring to Chefoo's position by the sea — with a Chinese seal, the special characters on which are intended to convey the meaning of 'Chefoo — Old Scholars' Association'. The crest was adopted in 1935, and its designer was Theo Hirst.

was rather a shock to surface and find two Japanese guards pointing their rifles right at them!

Usually, however, outings were less dare-devilish! The Second Beach was the place for 'cat's eyes' — parts of a little shell-fish which spiralled round a tiny 'door' to the inside. What fun to hunt for them in the warm sand — a nostalgic memory coupled in Chefusian thoughts with visits to the beach. In fact, at one stage, the boys made tieclips with the lustrous little shell.

A seaside highlight for the girls was a holiday trip to Lighthouse Island — combined, daringly, with the Boys' School! 'The boat journey was fraught with danger as some of the boys had scorpions (minus their stings but still an evil purplish colour) with which they chased various screaming girls! The island itself was idyllic — deep blue sea, white lighthouse and hills of golden sand. Some of us girls got into trouble after this particular picnic because we'd taken off our shoes and stockings to slide down the sand-banks — the height of immodesty and thoughtlessness!'

O CHEFOO SHORE

O Chefoo shore so bare and wild —
Meet school for a poetic child;
Land of brown hills and blinding blasts,
Land of slow junks and swaying masts,
Land of my youth! What mortal hand
Can e'er untie the grateful band
That knits me to thy sunny strand?
As I review each well known scene,
Think what is now and what has been,
My soul would fain as once of yore,
Stand on thy sunny shell-strewn shore.

(*Anon*)

Girls' crews 1920

Bare-legged time, in the early part of the century, was
only for rowing (in blouses with sailor collars and dark blue
skirts) or swimming (with red kerchiefs tied over their
heads to protect against the sun).

Even the little pink and white jelly-fish were part of
Chefoo life in those days. Summer holidays saw them flung
through the air by the boys, at those same scorpion-scared
screaming girls. Night time calmed the laughter but the
sea's magic was still there. The distant roar lulled Chefusians to sleep and more than once there was the thrill of a
swim in the moonlight. School leavers in the girls' sixth
form never forgot how the ocean gained a phosphorescent
quality as they let it stream through their fingers.

The islands in the bay, too, breathed a magic from the past. 'One year we went with Mr Duncan in a sampan to the Bluff and then sailed over to some of the islands between there and the lighthouse. I remember seeing the old cemetery over there which has graves of people who were shipwrecked out among those islands.' On the return trip did their thoughts run amok with visions of those graves? For when they should have been heading for the shore again, they noticed their light craft being blown further out to sea. There was nothing for it but to pull down the sails and attempt the very long row.

Sadly the sea trips did not always have happy endings. Tony was a day boy, whose father had a small cruiser with an outboard motor. The boy was sitting on the roof of the cabin when his hat blew off. Dad turned the boat round suddenly — Tony lost his balance and fell into the sea — his father dived in after him. Then the infamous Chefoo South Wind blew the light boat away from the swimmers, and both were drowned. The sea was a chameleon whose smooth polythene surface could prove treacherous.

The second quarter of the century had already started when the *S.S. Koyoda Maru 21* was on her way from Darien to Chefoo. Chefoo School teacher Mr Edwards was a passenger. At half past nine in the morning, he was standing on the deck with friends when the cry went up, 'Man overboard!' Sure enough, from the stern they could see a man's head in the water — rapidly receding from the ship. Without a moment's hesitation, Mr Edwards took off his coat and boots, preparing to dive to the rescue of the drowning Japanese.

Slowly the ship began to circle round and as the man's head appeared again, Mr Edwards plunged in . . . just in time, for when the ship's boat picked them both up, the Japanese was unconscious. Artificial respiration brought life again and so Mr Edwards warmly deserved the three ringing cheers Chefoo School gave when he was presented with a vellum, awarded by the Royal Humane Society for his gallantry and signed by HRH the Prince of Wales. Today a 1928 copy of 'Chefoo Daily News' is still available to read the story of Mr Edwards' bravery.

BOATING: AN IMPRESSION

The wind is from the northwest and the sea is rather choppy. The boatman has his trousers rolled high, but before he gets us away, he is wet to the waist. Safely out beyond the breakers, we pull a short way and are given the order to 'easy'; after many exhortations to good works we continue and paddle on towards the Bluff.

After a long spell we stop to rest our weary limbs, and we look around. Against the sky, a background of beautiful red and gold, Settlement Hill stands out very dark and clear-cut, looking twice as high as when seen from the land: it seems to be keeping watch over the city and harbour. It has just lighted the lamp in the Lighthouse, and the red of the lamp is no brighter than the sunset behind it. In the harbour entrance is a big junk bound for a distant port: all her dark brown sails are raised to the highest to catch what breeze there is, for the wind is dropping with the sun. The sun soon is below the horizon, and there only remains a soft pink and orange glow behind the city, partly veiled by the evening smoke from a thousand chimneys.

And so home to a well-earned rest: and one has the thought that it is worth joining the Boat Club if only to see a sunset like that.

AJC
(from *The Chefusian*, Summer Term 1934)

'Mr McLaren (Larry to us boys of course), a truly worthy Scot' was the centre of another piece of sea drama. 'He was short of stature and a poor swimmer, but full of courage and with a strong sense of duty. Once when a strong North Wind brought huge waves pounding on the sandy shore, only senior boys and strong swimmers were allowed to surf-bathe — but not even they without a master with them.

'Rather than deprive them of fun Larry, being on duty, went in. There was a strong undertow after each roller crashed on the sand. Larry was caught in this, lost his footing and was being rapidly swept out into deep water. Happily four of us seniors saw this, together lifted him above our heads and brought him ashore — step by step, as waves broke over us, leaving us gasping for breath in the intervals. Needless to say, he went up in our estimation.'

Summer holidays! Everyone stayed at Chefoo — distances to inland China made going home almost impossible. Days were filled with sunlight and sea. Sometimes mother and father would arrive to join in the holidays as a new little one in the family was ready to come to school. Reunited with Mum and Dad and a whole coastline to be explored . . . Golden mornings brought 'fantastic times of swimming in the ocean, diving from the raft, games in the water or lying on the beach looking for cat's eyes.'

Sun-drenched afternoons spelled CSSM. Sandy shores in so many parts of the world are familiar with that big red banner, its white letters indicating that here was a Children's Special Service Mission.

Special?

First the pulpit — built of sand, packed into place by sun-tanned hands and holiday spades, and decorated with pebbles forming a text against a background of flowers and greenery. Sandy seats were tackled next so that the 'congregation' could enjoy every comfort when the speaker took over the sand-cathedral.

Maybeth remembers it clearly. Her life at Chefoo was full of escapades as she led her dorm in adventures which gave the staff many a headache — midnight picnics in weird places where they were never caught, dangerous

ledge-walking on the outside of buildings in their nighties at dead of night. The staff resorted to prayer meetings just for her! Was Maybeth the reason Mr Godfrey Webb-Peploe came all the way from India to lead the CSSM meetings one year on the North China coast? Anyway, it was right there under a denim-blue sky, in the shadow of the sandy throne, that Maybeth surrendered her life to the Lord Jesus. Maybeth's penchant for fun and adventure never changed but her life had a new goal — to please her Saviour. God used those CSSM services to reach the children's hearts.

One yearly scene that beautiful spot witnessed was the baptismal service. It left a vivid impression on the candidates for baptism and the Chefusians who solemnly watched from the golden beach. Girls and boys who had trusted in the Lord Jesus for salvation came to the place in their lives when they wanted to tell the world. Baptism showed that they had thrown in their lot with the people of God. So staff members were informed and instruction from the Bible given.

Then the great day would arrive. The Chinese Church joined the CIM school and the baptism was by immersion in the sea. 'When the tide was low,' Kathryn recalls, 'it was a long walk out to sea where it was deep enough and each girl would hold the hand of a Chinese woman, also being baptized. Even in my teens, I felt the "specialness" of a healthy teenage girl holding the hand and supporting some frightened Chinese woman as she pushed through the water and then — coming back together.'

And so Chefoo School enjoyed the coastline right from the beginning of term. Not immediately before, though, for the journey on the ocean could be 'a painful experience, especially the rounding of the promontory at the place where two seas meet. That was calculated to take all the glamour from going to school!'

The sea! It added so much to life. One missionary parent wrote for the CIM magazine in 1937, 'One of the delightful things about Chefoo is that it is by the sea. Because CIM is an "inland" mission, most parents are in the interior for years at a time, and a place where there is a tang of salt in the air, where seagulls sail out over the water, and in the distance is always the lovely line of the sea horizon, seems the right place for children, for it puts them half-way towards the homelands. Besides, the sea is a good educator. It teaches the children to swim and most of them can do a mile before they leave. It teaches them to handle an oar or a rudder. It also brings to the school travellers who tell of London, California or Madagascar; experts who lecture on wireless, butterflies or aeroplanes; musicians who let the children hear first-class music; and, best of all, the sea in summer brings fathers and mothers to stay for a few weeks' holiday, whilst in winter it bears shiploads of children to different points along the coast from which they start on long journeys into the interior for their yearly visit home.'

The sea added . . . Sadly, the sea sometimes took away . . . But more than anything, it *gave* — fun, memories, a beached American ship, a whale and even . . .

'I had very few possessions,' David says, as the ocean prompted long-ago thoughts, 'because my parents were so very far away. But I did have this one rubber ball that I liked.'

One year it just worked out that David could go on vacation with the others at the end of term. Making the voyage to Kunming, they ran into a terrible storm on the Straits of Hainan. 'It felt like the boat was hitting bottom and every time the rear end came out, the propellor spun like mad.'

'Lord, if You just get me out of this,' prayed David, 'I'll give You . . . I'll give You . . . Why! I'll give You my ball!' Overboard went the precious treasure. Right away, David recalls, his fears were somewhat relieved. In fact he was the only member of the party who could face his supper!

'But can you imagine,' he continues, 'about six months later I was back at Chefoo, on the beach. Right at my feet, an identical ball rolled up! I immediately claimed it as my own. I felt the Lord had given me back my very own red rubber ball.'

And who knows? Perhaps, with the sea, He did.

OH TIME, TURN BACK!

I never see a stretch of sunlit beach
Without reverting to my childhood days
When on a China shore I knelt and sought
The buried 'Cats eyes' — stones with spiral base
And concaves of a dusty smoke or pink.
I slowly smoothed the coarse-grained sand in layers
And crawled upon my knees and smoothed again —
But had I known that in my later years
The width of oceans, circumstance and time
Would keep me from this pleasure that I took
For granted, I would have hoarded all I found,
For on no other beach can they be traced
That I have known. The austerity of Time!
'This hour I give, but ask me not again.'
Oh Time! — remorseless, miserly — turn back
And give me just one hour upon that sand!

      I never see a blue expanse of bay
      But that I picture junks with old patched sails
      That glide through China waters, guided by
      The giant eyes upon the bow to keep
      The devils from approaching — lazy, sluggish
      Junks and sampans — drowsy as the noon
      Of summer days. Oh, cool me with the punkas!
      Put upon my head an old pith helmet!
      Let me step into a waiting rickshaw!
      Oh Time! — turn back and give me just one hour
      Upon the China soil where I was born!

I never see a ship but that my heart
Cries out to board her — walk the sloping decks —
Spend hours against the railing, looking down
Into the blackness of night oceans. Strange,
The pull of masts and rigging — pitching, rolling
In the ebon sky — and stars that follow
Night by night. Oh Sea-Wind — blow across
My eager face again and let me feel
The salt of spray upon my lips and cheek!
Oh Time! — turn back and give me just one hour
Upon the China waters calling me!
                        Dorothy Loosley

FOUNDATION DAY
JUNE 15th

Timetable of events:

14th

Annual Boat Races in HERO and LEANDER — from the pier beyond the Second Beach to a finishing line in front of the Boys' School.

Usually two Boys' Crews and one Girls' Crew took part.

14th Evening
Bump Supper

15th a.m.

Cricket Match versus the 'Old Boys' (their team strengthened by such visitors as could be induced to play, some from the Western settlement in Chefoo)

Foundation Day Service in the Memorial Hall

15th p.m.
Tennis Tournament

Tea (and lemonade!) under the trees in the Boys' School Grounds (with a Garden Party atmosphere, brothers and sisters mingling freeely on this occasion)

Open Air Concert, after dark under the stars in the Boys' Quad (all quite romantic and exciting).

Doxology

A SONG FOR LEANDER AND HERO BOAT CLUBS

About 1938 the Boys' Boat Club was divided into two clubs, Hero and Leander.

Each club had its badge which we reproduced by lino-prints for the headings of the daily notices of crew-outings. The badges show Hero the priestess at her altar, and Leander diving into the Hellespont.

This song was written in July, 1941, inspired by races of that year, but since the publication of the song, enlivened with Mr Houghton's vigorous tune, Hero and Leander have never raced. Before June, 1942, the Japanese took over all the boats, and fishing parties used those sacred vessels.

The song had two versions, one for Hero to sing, and one for Leander. As both versions were sung at the same time, the resulting clash of words and rivalry was terrific.

Here is the "Hero Version":

Boys' crews, 1928

64

Leander swam to Hero long ago across the sea,
  And Hero and Leander still with loyal hearts we cherish.
Through weary weeks of training we have laboured
    zealously
  That Hero's glorious fame may never, never perish.

Chorus: So shout out for Hero, she waited by the sea,
      And her courage, her courage no disaster could
        diminish.
      In calm or in tempest courageous hearts have we,
      And we'll wait for Leander at the finish!

So when the harassed coxes lay us level at the start,
  And the race begins and the cox's voice on our heedless
    ears is dinning,
At forty strokes to the minute see us spurt with bursting
    heart —
  Past the Boathouse, past the Lido, we are winning, we
    are winning!

And when the race is over, win or lose, we disembark;
  Soon comes supper gay in the good old way, with cheery
    talk and faces,
And the speeches brief and the singing, and the bathing
    after dark,
  But the climax of the season is the Races, is the Races!

  Leander sings the same verses, except that in the last line
    of the first verse it will be 'Leander's glorious fame.'
    The chorus goes:

      So shout for Leander; Leander loved the sea;
      And his courage, his courage no disaster could
        diminish.
      In calm or in tempest courageous hearts have
        we,
      And triumphant we'll be leading at the finish.
                                            SGM

Drill displays

A SPOONFUL OF SUGAR MAKES THE MEDICINE GO DOWN

Foundation Day celebrations made the Summer Term one to be eagerly anticipated. But it was not the only feature colouring those bright weeks. The second great event of the school year, Exhibition Day, was held at the close of the Summer Term in July — a time specially chosen so that any parents who were holidaying in the Port of Chefoo could be present. Each of the three schools had its own day.

Songs, recitations, speeches and the actual prizes were given in the Memorial Hall. The Girls' School Programme was followed by a Drill Exhibition which took place on a tennis court. The boys' Drill Display, after their programme, was held in the Quad.

1934 was to be the last year of the record of *three* school programmes, for by 1935 a new era had started for the CIM schools. The *Chefoo Daily News* of August 7th, 1935 headed its reports 'End of Term Celebrations. CIM Preparatory School and — CIM *Co-Tuition* School'! It continues:

'Now comes the special joy of seeing the happy Prepites* emerge from the background of the platform and take their places. When the last little darling has taken her place, Dr Hoyte takes his place coolly and calmly on the platform, receiving an extra clap of welcome from those who know what a delightful chairman he will make.

'Now the audience becomes quiet as Dr Hoyte leads in a simple prayer of thanksgiving and intercession. As one glances up at the hundred children, one sees bowed heads and closed eyes and in many cases reverently folded little

---

* Children of the Prep School, aged 6 to 10.

hands, and one knows that the girls and boys are following Dr Hoyte's simply chosen words as their own prayer.

'The items of the programme are now to begin and we all settle down to enjoy them. It is not possible to comment on every item in a short space. The singing of the songs was really excellent.

'The enunciation was clear, and almost every word, even the first of every verse, could be distinctly heard. Was the piano-playing quite up to last year's standard? This was discussed afterwards. Nevertheless it was a great delight.

'Of the recitations, the "Seed Song", the "New Shoes" and the "Cats' Tea-Party" were especially charming. Is it because the children of the Primary are so simply natural and un-selfconscious, or are their recitations especially enjoyed because one is thinking of the parents far away who are unable to see their bairnies' performance? But apart from the charm of these recitations in themselves, the anticipation and keen enjoyment of the audience of little people on the platform was quite a part of the show for the grown-ups in the arena. Each child seemed to share in the recitations, whether of lighter or more serious strain. The programme closed with a fine rendering of the story of David and Goliath in the words of Scripture, which were clearly recited in a realistic manner.

'Now all eyes were turned on Dr Hoyte who rose to address the children. Nor were the grown-ups disappointed, his simple charm of manner in telling of the reminiscences of his childhood and the direct message of "do it with thy *might*" winning all hearts.

'Mrs Hoyte and Miss Kendon received a hearty clap as they took their places for the prize-giving, and it was the last pleasure of the afternoon to see the successful children come down and receive the reward of their year's steady work. A special clap, accompanied by stamping of feet, went to Dorothy Boxer who gained the Conduct Prize.

'And so another milestone in the annals of the Prep School has passed, and the little darlings whom Miss Kendon received into the Primary four years ago are now ready to be delivered to Miss Rice and Mr Bruce, and they are followed by the prayers not only of their fond parents

but by all of us who love little children and who desire the best and greatest for each life in years to come.'

* * *

'Do moderns read Charles Kingsley's *Water-Babies*? If not, they could hardly appreciate to the full the Cantata, founded on the classic story, which was the *pièce de résistance* on the second afternoon of the end-of-term celebrations at the CIM Schools. But no one who was there — and every available seat was occupied, the Prep School boys and girls being accommodated in seats outside the unglassed back-windows of the Memorial Hall — could fail to admire the competent rendering of music which was far from simple.

'Comparisons with previous years break down, because (as Mr P. A. Bruce, the Headmaster, pointed out in his introductory speech) the Boys' and Girls' Schools have become *one*, and therefore *two* Exhibitions would be anomalous. And so the usual procession of girls, incredibly fresh and demure in their white dresses and blue sashes, was followed immediately on to the platform by a procession of boys. Rumour has it that since the introduction of Co-Tuition the boys are becoming seriously concerned about keeping their hair in order. At any rate we have it from a reliable source that in one of the junior forms it was a liberal application of cold cream which secured glossy heads and straight partings!

'And now to come to the Cantata — in which, as we have hinted, boys as well as girls took part — we should like to pay a tribute first of all to Miss Rice who, seconded by Mr Stanley Houghton, spent many long hours in training the singers. They have a high standard, and we should not be surprised to hear that they were wholly satisfied with the result, but the audience showed unmistakable appreciation both of the chorus and of the soloists.

'The choruses were rendered sometimes by the girls or by the younger boys only, sometimes by selected groups. But we think most people would agree that those in which the whole school participated made the strongest appeal. For these choruses a special and most effective bass part had been written by Mr S. Houghton.

'The company then adjourned to the new Co-Tuition Building to inspect the handwork, which included some very telling posters, designs for book-covers, etc. One room was devoted to needlework and dressmaking, in which (so far as we know) the boys have no part, and another to a remarkably fine display of book-rests, chess-boards and nicknacks of all sorts, carved in wood and suitably varnished. In view of the fact that this subject was added to the curriculum only a year ago, the results reflect considerable credit on teachers and taught alike.'

CIM SCHOOLS PRIZE-GIVING

'July 31 was the third and last day of the end-of-term celebrations at the CIM School. The actual distribution of prizes was preceded by music and recitations. The Headmaster, Mr P. A. Bruce, MA., presented a very interesting report of the year's work. It was, he said, the first year of an important new experiment, namely Co-education. There was no doubt that the great majority of the boys and girls approved of it, and as for the staff their worst fears had not been realized and they were constantly discovering fresh advantages in the system. By using this method and through the provision of the new buildings they were able to divide each form into A and B divisions, boys and girls with average brains took their place in the B division and could thus receive more individual attention, while those in the A division with unusual mental endowments were not held back by the less brilliant members of the same form. Grading was possible in all subjects, e.g. a boy might have, as it were, an A brain for mathematics and a B brain for languages, and moreover it was always possible to rise from the lower division to the higher, if that seemed advisable. Mr Bruce referred in modest terms to the excellent result of the Oxford examinations last year. Although the whole form sat for these exams, without any special selection on the part of the staff, fifteen boys and girls out of eighteen passed the School Certificate, eight of them obtaining exemption from matriculation, while in the Junior exam there were only two failures amongst twenty-five entries, and nine obtained honours.

'It was impossible to omit a reference to the *Tungchow** piracy, an experience which had enabled them all, especially those on the staff itself, to prove the goodness and power of God. Finally Mr Bruce paid a tribute to the housekeepers, wardrobe-keepers, matrons, nurses and to Dr Judd, by whose constant watchfulness the health of the boys and girls had been maintained and the inevitable epidemics had nearly always been confined to one of the three schools.'

*　　　*　　　*

Another 'spoonful of sugar', this time in the Spring Term, was *The Cake Match*, a special six-a-side soccer game. Ben's precious diary from the early nineteen hundreds, recounts the excitement and fun of that annual event:

'Thursday, March 28th 1912
The semi-final Cake Match was played this afternoon and I rejoice to say that Hunt's side won so I will play in the final with Dorothy and the other girls and crowds of people watching on. The cake will be on a stand beside the field in front of our very eyes when we play the final. It will be played on Saturday after next.

　　This is the result so far:—
　　Hunt I v Smith or Evans
The match between Smith and Evans will come off on

* See page 41

71

'Cake Match' final, 1912 (winning team in front row)

Tuesday next.
The weather was fine today. Very little breeze today.

April 6th
I am now suffering joyfully from an over amount of cake inside of me. This is the result of a lot of hard-fought games. In plainer words Hunt's team was victorious in the final cake-match and received the cake. It was a huge three-layered cake about two feet high by two feet in diameter at the base. The top layer was only about five inches in diameter and was given to the referee.

After the match a photograph was taken: first of the winning team, then of both teams together.'

*   *   *

Many years throughout the Chefoo Schools' century have seen another event — a Cross Country run. In China days the boys ran from the Black Dragon Temple over hill and gully for approximately two and a half miles. All the non-participants plus the staffs and pupils of the Girls' and Prep Schools would be at the finishing line to cheer the runners in.

Later in his diary, Ben was to write 'I am glad I have taken the trouble to keep this Journal of Chefoozian pleasure (and otherwise).' This extract makes one wonder if the Cross Country could possibly be one of the 'pleasures'!

'On Wednesday (April 16th) the long run came off. We left the school for the monastery at 2.15 p.m. We were ready to run down for about 3 o'clock . . . At last my turn came and I started off chasing after Södabom who was in front of me. After a long chase along the stoney watercourse I caught Södabom up and passed him. He, however, kept close on my heels and I was hardpressed. Once I stumbled and fell but, fearful that he would catch me up, I got up and rushed on. Soon we came upon Emslie who started 15 seconds before Södabom. I followed hard after Emslie but he led me a little longer way and Södabom rushed on by a shorter way. I passed Emslie. Then, after climbing a gully, I heard Tim McCarthy gaining on me from behind. I raced on harder and climbed down and out of another gully but Tim passed me. After a while I came to the high road and rushed along it. Soon I heard Ray McCarthy coming up and he soon passed me. Then Emslie came up again to me racing with all his might. I made up my mind I would not let him pass me. We raced together for a long time. Once I made a sudden turn and tripped across his legs and fell head first down a steep incline. I quickly jumped to my feet (only being a little scratched) and rushed on, still in the lead. I jumped over a fence and made straight for the school. Emslie tried hard to catch me up several times. Then as we neared the audience he made a final spurt. I threw back my head and put my last ounce of strength into it, determined not to be caught up before the girls, and came into the porch one second before Emslie. Then I fell down in a heap and could only with difficulty get up and put my cloak on.'

One Field Day, also in the first quarter of the twentieth century, an unusual and dramatic incident happened which turned the Chefusians — staff and pupils — into one huge Debating Society! Who won the race that year? That was the question. Vivian outlines the event: 'Cricket, soccer, field hockey, rounders, swimming, rowing, jumping and most of all — running, were activities I just loved,' he says. 'One day there was an Old Boys' Field Day and competition with the Boys' School. An old boy, by the name of Malcolm, was running in the 440 yards. Properly run it is the toughest of all races — a sprint all the way. Malcolm ran magnificently and was way out in front but, I guess, he was not in the very best condition. A yard or two before the finishing line, he collapsed and slid *under* the tape without "breasting" it.

'The judges had a great hassle — had he or had he not complied with the rules? They decided against him and I have never forgotten the excitement and drama of the race and its climax. I've often used this incident as an illustration in speaking when referring to 2 Timothy 2.5' ('Follow the Lord's rules for doing his work, just as an athlete either follows the rules or is disqualified and wins no prize.' Living Bible).

*　　*　　*

A totally different character of the same era *and* with the same name figures in an amusing classroom adventure. The *master* this time was Mr Malcolm and he was having trouble with a Fifth Form boy who is now a surgeon. At this time, however, the boy was not displaying his academic brilliance. It was a halcyon Chefoo summer day. In the classroom the French doors lay open to the sun but the master was less than sunny-tempered with the surgeon-to-be. At last the offending pupil decided he'd had enough — enough of French, enough of school, enough of Chefoo altogether. There and then he ran away. He was good at sports and wasted no time.

74

Mr Malcolm gazed at the open door. After a pause, he took after the fugitive — much to the delight of the class. The chuckling subsided rather dramatically, though, when the master returned holding the pupil by the scruff of the neck. He had caught him before he had reached the front gate!

That was the end of classroom studies for one afternoon. Instead, a spellbound group of boys, who never again gave Mr Malcolm any problems, heard of their master's exploits in his early years. 'I guess you didn't know I was the champion runner of New Zealand!' he began . . .

Boys' School 1906

MORTAR BOARD AND GOWN

It was the year 1910. Halley's comet was at its height in the Chinese evening sky. 'One memory I have of that stays with me', recalls Carrington. 'Mrs McCarthy escorted some of us up to the roof of the school to have a look. It was spectacular. I secretly hoped than that I would see it 76 years later. I wonder will I?'

Sixty-six years slipped by. In Chefoo School in Malaysia the top class was having a Creative English lesson. It was the dry season, and the weather, even in the mountains, was sunny and hot. Suddenly the jungle to the south side of the school was ablaze. Out hurried the class with their teacher and soon the whole school was gazing awestricken at another spectacular sight. Fresh from the scene, adjectives and similes tumbling naturally on to their pages, the class produced some of their best work ever.

'When news came round that the fire was out of control', wrote Julie, 'that's when the real tingle of excitement began. Excitement bubbled up and up like a pot of soup left on the stove which no one's looking after! The brilliant glistening of leaves waving in the blaze was ambushed calmly by angry, huge sticks of flame craving for more fuel.'

Ten-year-old Linda added, 'The next day we visited the smouldering heap. The ebony-coloured stumps against the sky looked like pencil lead on blue paper . . . In a way it had been worth it. I mean — it is not every day you get out of school early, is it?'

The birth of baby goats, landslides along the mountain road, a helicopter gliding through a gap in the jungle greenery to land on their very own playing field, a troupe of monkeys announcing their sudden presence with loud whoops in the trees — throughout the century so many unusual incidents have contributed to the rich educational heritage that was to belong to all Chefusians.

Perhaps the greatest educational experience of all was the thrill of passing the 'Oxford Examination' in China days. This was *the* great goal which drove teachers and pupils to a highly competitive standard of education. 'The Oxford Certificate is what impressed the University of Maryland. You betcha!' wrote one American of his graduating qualifications from Chefoo in 1925. Year after year the sixth formers covered themselves in glory, from as early as 1908. *China's Millions* began to carry little reports of this nature:

'The publication of the results of the recent Oxford Local Examination has again caused jubilation among the scholars and teachers at the Chefoo Schools. Of the 42 pupils who sat for this examination last summer, all have been successful' (1913).

The mission was delighted. The school staff was delighted. What about the MKs*? Ben's schoolboy jottings of nearly 70 years ago reveal a boy's perspective on that jubilant CIM report:

'Wednesday, September 17th, 1913
Poor old diary, you have been neglected haven't you. Well, we had the Ox. exams (since I last wrote in you, and the summer hols) . . . School began on September 2nd. I have become a prefect this term . . ..

Tuesday, October 14th
Yesterday morning I had a very painful stomach-ache and stayed upstairs all morning. I ate no breakfast. After which dinner time came and the boys marched into the dining-room. I was still upstairs. Suddenly I heard a terrific shout come from the dining-room. I knew that shout from every other shout I have ever heard: the results had come! I was trembling with excitement. I rushed down a flight of back stairs which brought me on to the opposite side of the quad from the dining-room. I heard shout after shout . . . I heard my name mentioned with several other names. I was wild with excitement. I rushed back up the

* 'missionary kids'.

78

stairs and around to another flight which led to the dining-room. Here Squashus met me. He told me that the results were fine, no one had failed, out of the 42 candidates 23 had honours and I had third class honours. We had yesterday free from school and are going to have the whole of Wednesday which is half-holiday anyway.

Wednesday, October 15th

I forgot to finish telling of what happened on Monday. After dinner I went downstairs to the reading room. Suddenly two sturdy fellows rushed in and picked me up on their shoulders and ran out again into the quad. Soon the whole school was around me and under me and carried me all around the quad. Then they let me down . . . It must not be supposed that only I was carried about, as nearly all who got honours and are still at school had their turns. Theodor Wilder was eighth in the whole world in merit among all who took the Oxford Senior Exam.'

Unfortunately, in that land of monks and poets in which they were growing up, the Chefusians were denied education in one specific area — learning to speak the Chinese language and explore the culture of the great Chinese civilization.

A distinguished old boy wrote, 'I have long been critical of the fact that no one at Chefoo taught us about the land of our birth. The result was that, arriving in the USA aged 16, and asked about the language, history and civilization of China, I was tongue-tied.'

A university professor adds, 'CIM children were totally deprived of a chance to study Chinese language or culture . . . Without exaggeration I would estimate that every Chefoo graduate of my period, trained to use English and Chinese bilingually, could have earned at least $25,000 per annum for the past forty years and consulted with corporation presidents, cabinet ministers or general staff officers. In fact, many of them have barely struggled to the level of junior clerks or country school teachers, and two of my close friends have committed suicide in bitter frustration.'

'What a glorious chapter,' comments another, 'could be written if they had taught Chinese at Chefoo.'

It seems a short-sighted policy, but the staff weren't to know then how valuable an asset a knowledge of Chinese would be now. 'I believe the question of learning Chinese was faced,' wrote one teacher of those days, 'but we felt that our main aim was to prepare the children for life in the *homeland*. The Port of Chefoo did not boast cultural amenities and the Chinese there were working-class people. We did not deem it wise to encourage the speaking of the language nor even think it might be possible to engage a qualified teacher. One would need to know the times and conditions to appreciate this.' It is interesting to note that an American mission school near Peking didn't teach Chinese either.

One English old boy recounts, 'Pupils were not allowed to speak Chinese. How dated this concept seems now. Was it for fear of contamination? Naturally we boys learned to swear in Chinese and on one occasion, as a Chinese walked by the wall, some boys swore at him — at comprehensive length! He turned out to be the senior Chinese of the compound and went straight to the headmaster . . .'

Chris wrote in the CSA magazine later, 'We lived a very sheltered type of life in the mission compound. We were protected from being polluted by the servants by being forbidden to converse with them in Chinese. Thus we forgot all the Chinese which we learnt in our younger days. (How many Chefusians were sorry for this loss of their knowledge of the Chinese language?)'

Another old boy, whose lineage goes right back to Chefoo's earliest days, certainly feels this way. 'It was in relation to this fact of its location', he writes, 'that I think Chefoo let us down most lamentably. Contact with the Chinese was almost taboo, lest we be corrupted! There was hardly one member of the staff or the Chefoo community who took the trouble to teach us about the people among whom we lived — we learnt nothing about their history, their civilization, their religion or their art — we 'did' the Yellow River for geography and that is about as far as it went.

'Ashamed as I am about my lack of real knowledge of the Chinese', he continues thoughtfully, 'I have the most vivid recollection of the country itself. I recall in minute detail every fold of the hills, every wild flower to be found on them, every bug and beetle and butterfly, the colours of the sea, the smell of the South wind in June, the bitterness of January and February, the farms and the temples. These things are "Chefoo" to me — not the School.'

As the century marched forward towards World War II, things began to change. Certainly the fact that Chefoo School mingled with the world in Internment Camp contributed to an about-face. 'Weihsien was very good for the staff at Chefoo,' an Australian ventured to say. 'It at

SCHOOL BALLAD

In eighteen hundred and eighty one
The Chefoo School was just begun
The finest school beneath the sun
   Chefoo, Chefoo for ever.

Chorus: Schoolwork and tennis and cricket and tea
          Boating and swimming in the sea
          Football and hockey and sports for me
             Chefoo, Chefoo for ever.

In eighteen hundred and eighty two
They started cricket at Chefoo
And beards and toppers improved the view
   Chefoo, Chefoo for ever.

In eighteen hundred and eighty three
Football began with brutal glee
And shins were battered and ankle and knee
   Chefoo, Chefoo for ever.

In eighteen hundred and eighty four
They rowed boat races along the shore
And backs did ache and hands were sore
   Chefoo, Chefoo for ever.

In eighteen hundred and ninety six
They built the School of stone and bricks
And the boys got up to tricks
   Chefoo, Chefoo for ever.

In nineteen hundred and thirty see
McCarthy welcome P.A.B.
They are jolly good fellows, and so say we
    Chefoo, Chefoo for ever.

In nineteen hundred and thirty four
The sexes segregate no more
Co-eds the scheme for evermore
    Chefoo, Chefoo for ever.

In nineteen hundred and thirty five
The pirates captured us alive
But British 'planes drove off the hive
    Chefoo, Chefoo for ever.

In nineteen hundred and forty two
They swiped our School and compound too
But still we stayed in our Chefoo
    Chefoo, Chefoo for ever.

In nineteen hundred and forty three
They made us shift and travel by sea
And we came to Weihsien C.A.C.
    Chefoo, Chefoo for ever.

In nineteen hundred and forty four
We hope to return to the well known shore
Our School's the same for ever more
    Chefoo, Chefoo for ever.

least got them into the twentieth century.' Since that turn-around things have been different. Chinese lessons started at Chefoo School, Kuling.

Despite the sad lack of local environmental studies, Chefoo bred men and women of distinguished ability. Among those who have received prominence are university professors, doctors, politicians, authors, churchmen, lawyers and sportsmen.

CIM and OMF have been proud of those who have achieved academic brilliance, as this little report from the *China's Millions* of 1909 shows:

'George King . . . has recently taken his MB ChB of Edinburgh, graduating First Class with Honours. He took medals in five subjects and First Class Honours in all. As an old Chefoo scholar, we offer him our congratulations and for all the successes of the sons and daughters of workers . . . we give God thanks.'

But, as a Canadian old girl points out, 'One realizes that a number of Chefusians have achieved prominence in areas of public life, careers and sports, to whom honour is due, but I also like to think of those who because of health were not able to serve, for example, on the mission field as desired, but who either patiently taught at home, or filled a useful editorial post for over forty years on a Christian paper, or, when gifted in writing and speaking in four languages, cared for an aging mother faithfully.' However, several hundred are today in full-time Christian work.

The old description of Chefoo as 'the best school East of Suez' had a ring of truth about it.

DID YOU HEAR THE ONE ABOUT . . .?

'Boy, take your seat,' Mr Lindsay called for he had spotted Clarke crawling around during Prep.

'Yes sir! Where to?' Clarke replied, lifting his bench.

'Discipline was sometimes . . . er, inefficient,' explains Parry Tertius, who was a pupil from 1896 to 1906, including his first two years at Tongshin where the Prep School began. 'Mr Lindsay was a perfect gentleman and the boys were not angels. We knew whom we could cheek!'

'I remember,' chuckles Chris, 'in the 1920s, Mr Duncan taking a Latin lesson in the Sixth Form. When he translated he had the habit of tipping his chair back against the wall. One day we moved his desk and chair forward, so that when he leant back he missed the wall and went flat on his back on the floor. He never faltered in his translation of the Latin, going straight on as if nothing had happened while he resumed his upright position. He knew we'd done it and we knew he knew but he had a very wry sense of humour and there was a twinkle in his eye.'

Arnold adds, 'Chefoo and my parents laid down an excellent foundation in the Scriptures on the way that I should go, but this did not remove from me that sinful streak which is common to mankind. One day when a master in the Boys' School, to whom we were all particularly averse, had turned his back to write on the blackboard, I dipped my pen in the inkwell and showered his clean linen suit with blobs of ink. Later when I went to China as a missionary, he became one of my prayer partners! I failed to apologize to him while he was on earth but fully intend that one of my first jobs in heaven will be to seek him out and express my regret . . .'

'During the 1914-18 war,' recalls one Chefusian from Australia, 'the Boys' School playground was alerted by a boy calling out, "Here's the Austrian Consul's car coming!" We stood on the wall overlooking the Beach Road. "Let's stone the car!" suggested one. By the time that little incident was reported and a few canings administered, there were no further stoning escapades!'

Consuls came to the fore in other circumstances, too — fortunately in a more favourable light. July 4th was the day the American Consul took the boys from the States for a launch trip round the bay and to the islands. This led to a fair bit of wrestling in the quad the following day when the British took out their envious feelings on their friends from America. However, Empire Day in May was their turn; all the children were taken on an outing.

Warfare in the playground did not usually stem from nationalistic feelings but from loyalty to their own gang. The boys had two notorious groups, the Jolly Rovers and the War Arrows. Intense rivalry developed between these two gangs in the early part of the century, and their scouting expeditions sometimes resulted in a pitched battle near the trenches dug during an earlier war. These were mainly wrestling matches until one side could subdue the other. 'One great fight,' writes an old boy, 'was reminiscent of Homer's Battle of Troy!' Another American says, 'I was a Jolly Rover. Our large flag was red with a huge white skull and crossbones on it. The War Arrows had a white flag with crossed black arrows. The rivalry was terrific, occasionally winding up in fights in the hills where we would meet each other while conducting our manoeuvres.'

Later, it seemed right to the powers-that-be to have these 'scouting groups' disbanded. Houses were formed to take their place and school activities then became competitive between the more Christian tribes of Paton, Livingstone, Carey and Morrison!

* * *

Watching the cadets drilling at the Chinese Military Academy one day, a group of boys hid behind the wall ready to throw a spanner in the works.

CHINA INLAND MISSION COMPOUND :
CHEFOO 1931.

Scale : 183' : 1"
Roads & Paths :
Gullies :
Embankments :
Tennis Courts :

B.S.: Boys' School
G.S.: Girls' "
P.S.: Preparatory "
a : Private Residences
b : G.S. Playground
c : Chinese Church
d : Prayer Room

MILE ROAD

LILY DOUTHWAITE
(CHINESE)
HOSPITAL

BOYS' SCHOOL FIELD

BATHING HOUSE

BOAT HOUSE

Flagstaff

B S

N

DR. HOSPITAL

BUSINESS DEPT.

G.S.

Flagstaff

GIRLS' SCHOOL FIELD

SAN.

THE GINGERBREAD HOUSE

MEMORIAL HALL

Flagstaff

P.S.

SAN LANE

BATHING

PS

GS

BATHING

BEACH ROAD

'*Ki-boo-tso*' ('Forward march'), shouted the Drill Instructor.

Five seconds later a yell issued from behind the wall, '*Li-poo-ting*' ('About face')! Result — confusion among the cadets! Spotted, the boys fled down the hill chased by angry cadets. But the Chefusians knew every short cut and easily outdistanced their pursuers. This little venture was such a success that it was indulged in more than once and sometimes a complaint would reach the Head's ears, resulting in a 'gating'.

'During the winter holidays,' Roger remembers, 'two or three of us would hike to the Black Dragon Temple. This monastery was in a steep ravine back of the hill about three or four miles from the school. We would enter the temple and beat the brass gongs in front of the huge statue of Buddha and then tear out of the temple, across the bridge and up the steep hills with several irate monks after us!'

That particular group of Chefusians who honoured the school with their presence around 1920, were up to every prank they could think of. Their explanation is, 'We were not supposed to go without permission . . . and as we would not receive permission if we asked, we merely forgot to ask!' Such adventures as climbing down the ivy from their second-floor dormitories and silently sneaking out of the grounds for a midnight swim or a visit to the Chinese quarter of Chefoo, helped to liven up what one called a 'grey' existence. 'Occasionally we were caught,' one recalls, 'as sometimes the master on duty might conduct an unheralded bed-check on the dormitories, thus signalling a reception committee on our return. Outside a one-foot-wide ledge skirted the second floor of the Boys' School, and many times we climbed out the windows and on to the ledge and crawled to the other dormitories where we conducted night raids. We boys did have a real bagful of obnoxious tricks . . .'

'How those boys were controlled out of school hours,' says Mrs Butler, 'I cannot imagine. I heard one parent state when giving out the good conduct prize for the Boys' School, that all the boys were bad, as far as he could gather, so this prize must be for the one who was less bad than all the others.'

Amusing memories fill many a girl's thoughts too. 'I remember asking Miss Dobson once,' said a letter which came from the Philippines, 'what she would do if she heard strange noises at night! It was holiday time, and she said, "I'd turn over and go to sleep!" We took advantage of this and had a midnight party up in the prefects' room. It was windy that night, and just as well, for we had a very hard time keeping quiet . . . We got away with our prank, but another time the MKs weren't so lucky.'

'Some Sundays,' remembers Maybeth, 'a big boring man preached at Temple Hill Church. He was rather huge and had the habit of continually saying "er . . ." all through his sermons. We would count the "ers". Finally we called him Mr Blind Unbelief, because the verse of a hymn we often sang ran,

"Blind unbelief is sure to err
And take God's name in vain".'

Grace, who was a Chefusian during the Second World War, recounts, 'We were singing the hymn, "Lo! He comes with clouds descending," in which the chorus goes "Deeply wailing" three times and "Hallelujah" once. As we melodiously gave voice Miss Rice saw Lydia misbehaving. Leaving her hymnbook behind she strode towards her victim, through desks, scattering girls to right and left. She grabbed her just as we reached "Deeply wailing", but in triumph joined in the final "Hallelujah"!'

'Something stands out in my memory,' adds Mabel. 'Someone, who shall be nameless, was dared to march into Evening Service in the Memorial Hall with her coat inside out. And she did it — modelling brilliant blue brocade lining!'

A doctor from South Africa writes, 'Rabbits and other pets were kept at times. Like a number of friends I had a small scorpion in a tin which I took to church once in the Memorial Hall and which I last saw out of reach, two pews away, making good speed along the floor. Wires, batteries and torch bulbs were another way of spending time in church but I do not think we were any more irreligious than most horrible brats of the same age!'

*   *   *

'Amongst memorable "characters" at Chefoo China,' an Australian recalls, 'were several of the Chinese domestic staff. The head servant, an outstandingly genial personality with a gracious smile, was nicknamed *Zerubbabel* due to his small rotund figure.

'Kansampandi was in charge of the boats and the boys' changing rooms in the summer season. In winter, however, he was responsible for domestic heating and in particular for the coal fires in the classrooms which he tended between classes. Knowing that the whole class always stood when the teacher entered the room, he delighted in simulating the teacher by raising and lowering his shovel as a sign for the boys to rise and to be seated, causing as much amusement to himself as to the class.'

The good-mannered customs of the mid-century school made one old boy, a Londoner, remark 'The education was excellent but I learned to call everybody "Sir" including the school barber!'

Zerubbabel (left) and Kansampandi

'I remember,' an American writes, 'the times we acquired a little Chinese money and purchased *ru-bowdtzes* (small meat patties in flour). There were some roadside stalls on the Mule Road and we used to haggle with the merchants for more "goodies" than we had change for. The *ru-bowdtzes* were absolutely delicious.'

At that time, early in the century, peanut butter was as great a Chefoo speciality as it is today. 'There was a back room,' remembers Roger, 'where one of the Chinese employees made peanut butter all day long. Peanut butter was one of Chefoo School's main food items, being fed to us daily on bread. We could hide out back of the Peanut Butter Room and when the servant left for a few minutes, we would dart in and reach both hands into the enormous vats of freshly-made peanut butter, and fill our pants pockets with a pound or two and high-tail it out of there. We would eat this solid peanut butter to our hearts' content and barter the remainder back at school. Sometimes we had tummy aches and naturally our pants pockets were a mess!'

One Chefusian of the 1970s says, 'I went to school in the Cameron Highlands, Malaysia and to this day I don't consider a table properly set without a jar of crunchy *peanut butter*!'

'Thinking of food,' writes an English lady who went to school just before World War II, 'I wonder if I'm right in my theory about Bread and Scrape. Surely our bread slices must have been stacked prior to tea and then syrup *poured* over the top? How else could one account for some pieces being soaked with syrup and others only catching it at the corners or odd places?'

'As for the lukewarm, diluted drink called tea,' another from earlier in the century recalls, 'that was known by all the boys as gully water as it resembled the dirty creek water and tasted about the same! Gully water, rice porridge, bread and peanut butter and you about have the menu.'

However, a Canadian of the same vintage seems to think it was a reasonably wholesome diet on the whole and that upset stomachs occurred due to too much food at a sitting. 'The "cure" for this was simple but effective,' Stan says.

'The headmistress, who operated Sick Bay, used to examine the victim briefly to make sure he was not actually dying. Being assured on this point, she would give him a liberal dose of castor oil and tell him to go to bed.' Thirty-six hours of starvation and boredom soon put him right, and he was sent back to his lessons with the stern instruction 'Don't eat so much after this.'

*   *   *

'The last time I saw our old Head, Mr McCarthy,' Robert remembers, 'I was standing at Beehive Corner in Adelaide in 1921. I was waiting for my wife-to-be when Mr and Mrs McCarthy walked up from the railway station. We recognized each other and during the conversation I mentioned I was to be married the following evening at Northgate Street Baptist Church. Mr and Mrs McCarthy were both at the wedding, and Mrs McCarthy played the organ. One of those strange happenings verging on the miraculous.'

Was it prescience of a story like this that made me wonder if *romance* was part of life at Chefoo, China. Ruth wrote in reply, 'Romance? If by that you mean what is usually meant, you *have* to be kidding! Did you know that one of the worst crimes in the book was to talk to a boy other than your brother, always supposing you could get within yodelling distance of one? There were those who fancied someone in the other school, but any communication was virtually impossible. Of course, there was the highly illegal practice of swapping brothers on the one-and-a-half mile walk home from the Union Church, not so dangerous at the head of the crocodile as the teacher at the end who might know the girls intimately would not be so familiar with the rear view of their brothers. This scheme was limited to the better-planned families, however. A girl of sixteen with an eight-year-old brother did not find a ready market!'

From an early age these difficulties weighed heavily on Chefusians. One little eight-year-old girl wrote home to her parents, 'There are many problems in the world today. Why, we don't even know who we are going to marry.'

The considered opinion of some was that they'd never

Brothers and sisters walking together on the tennis court

marry anybody. Chefoo School was proving to be a poor preparation for social contact with the opposite sex. 'Talk about "apartheid",' says one. 'This was it!' And it bred naiveté rather than *savoir faire*.

Kathryn admits to the following little vignette. 'You have probably been told of the strict segregation between Boys' School and Girls' School; though Sunday evening service was held in the Boys' School Assembly Room, sitting in desks tightly crushed together, and girls looking carefully to the right and boys to the left — except, of course, for the brave ones who could not be seen by the accompanying staff member. There were rumours of clandestine meetings, arranged when sisters and brothers met each other on Saturday. My nearest approach to such was a tiny piece of paper, folded over and over. I opened it in a corner of the classroom and found written on it, "I am after you, are you after me?" I wonder now why I did not follow it up!'

'I think we all had our heroes in the Boys' School,' says

Mabel, 'and a smile across the aisle in the Memorial Hall or watching a cricket match sent us into ecstasies.'

But things weren't quite a hundred percent grim, only nearly! Romances like Henry's and Mary's cropped up — they were married in the Chefoo Assembly Hall in 1938. And 'though this is only hearsay,' writes Olga, 'our Maths teacher found his future wife in our class! He was the teacher, she was one of the pupils and a year or so later they were married.'

Early in 1937 a severe epidemic of measles hit Chefoo School. German measles was raging at the same time and the sick room was full. 'Dr Judd was nearly run off his feet,' writes Mary from New Zealand, and she would know, for she was the Prep School nurse. Help was urgently required, and arrived in the person of an eligible young doctor on his first term of service as a missionary. Mary the nurse got along famously with the new doctor, so well in fact that an engagement and than a wedding were in the offing. The harassed Dr Judd married them both in the Memorial Hall. 'After a short honeymoon,' concludes Mary, 'we returned to Chefoo to take over the medical work from Dr and Mrs Judd.'

Ewan and Priscilla were both teachers at the Kuling Chefoo School. Everyone there felt part of their romance. And to tidy everything up into neat little compartments, they sent their children to Chefoo School, Malaysia.

'Without straining my memory too much,' writes Allison from Australia, 'I can remember at least seven "matches" which materialized . . .'

The little church in the Cameron Highlands keeps the record right up to date by witnessing Don and Margie's fairytale wedding in 1979 — two Chefoo Malaysia teachers whom the school rather unwillingly spared for refugee work on Kampuchea's borders. Margie herself had been a Chefoo girl in the Philippines.

So staff romances throughout the century have been the 'in' thing — but instead of descending to the cultivation of romantic notions the girls of Chefoo Port days were encouraged to be *nice*. Printed and framed for their edification was this list:

Nice People Never . . .
   enter a room without knocking
   make fun of a foreigner's language
   make fun of people's disabilities
   talk when two people are talking
   talk when people are singing or playing a musical
      instrument
   get between the viewer and the shop window
   pick their teeth at table

(Although, Beth says, this last item was not hard to observe
as they had no toothpicks!)

One of Peggy's treasures is the following letter which, she
says, aptly illustrates with realism and humour the
traumatic experiences they endured on first leaving school
and being thrust into such a different world . . .

20th February 1926
'Are you becoming very worldly wise, oh Peggoty of
Chefoo origin? I don't know if I ever told you of how I
learned to swear — like the famous troopers swear, you
know.

Well, when I first entered hospital I though I knew all
there was to know, and I thought the worst word in
swearing circles began with D, and went on till it came to
N. This word was used very freely, I found, but it didn't
worry me particularly. And it came to pass on a day that I
was sponging an old Irish dad, and being "wash-all-over
night" his feet were doomed from the start. But how should
I know that he was ticklish on the soles of his feet? And each
time I got anywhere near he drew back his foot and said
B...... And the ward roared — men, nurses and myself.

And I got to his foot again, and the performance was
repeated with the same mirthful result.

After duty I was telling the yarn to my immediate pals,
using this ill-fated word quite freely — and there was a
visitor there too — until finally one of my pals told me very
seriously that I *must* not use that word. Only the lowest of
the low used it, and it was so vile as never to be written on
paper.

After I had finished nearly dying, I set a very close watch to my lips and I looked twice at every new word that was thrust upon my ears.

While I was busy doing that a man gave me two newspapers — *The Sporting Globe* and *The Truth*. Being brought up at Chefoo I put the Globe to one side. I had "morning time" the next day — Sunday — and I said "Oh fag — I won't go to church, I'll stay at home and read *The Truth*.

So I stayed, and I read. There was, I remember, a vivid description of a shipwreck where the crew rowed ashore to an uninhabited island kind of a place, and ate each other for meals . . . and as I read, thinking it a very detailed account indeed for a newspaper, in came a friend . . .

Well, I soon understood that *The Truth* was *not* read, and if it were merely touched, it would be advisable to wash the hands — and so on, and so forth. So I began to think life a very precarious venture. But how should a Chefooite know? Now my proposal is to send out a little

Nice People Never . . .
1   Use the following words — with a complete list of same
2   Read *The Truth*
3   Use wrong words in wrong places, or with wrong pronunciation, while acting the fool, thus making themselves liable to using the worst expressions (as one old girl did)
4   Make a fool of themselves generally
To be hung in a conspicuous place.'

                    With much love from a worldly wiseman
                    *   *   *

'We never questioned the decrees of our elders and betters,' another Australian old girl relates. 'We dimly felt that Miss Jones was onmiscient and clearly had X-ray vision. Miss Jones knew who had a hole in the toe of her stocking or was wearing a pin in lieu of a button (a crime), however these deficiencies were hidden from normal human eyes. You wouldn't presume to tell Miss Jones anything. She was one of the most amazing people I ever met. In the sewing women's workroom she had a motto on the wall, "Let everything be done decently and in order". This used to intrigue me, as the *amahs* knew no English and no one needed that exhortation less than Miss Jones!'

Contie, an old girl from England writing also about the second decade of the century, asks, 'Who remembers the floor scrubbing campaign which our third form carried out, and which we made last long past bed-time by swilling as many buckets of water over it as possible?

'The reason was that in order to go from door to window in one swooping glide, we had shaved birthday-cake candles on the floor beside our desks to rub the soles of our shoes slippery.

'Unfortunately we had not foreseen that Miss Jones would be giving out needles during a sewing lesson in the evening while we were doing our prep in the schoolroom. She had a painful fall with needles embedded in her hand.

'The scolding was firm and severe and well deserved, but while wielding our well-soaped scrubbing brushes some of us, peeping upside down through our legs astride, caught a glimpse of Miss Pyle and Mrs Knight in the doorway, suppressing mirth at the sight of our energy and zeal.

'In order to liven up one evening,' she continues, 'I balanced a soap-dish filled with water on the partially-open bedroom door, hoping to catch an unwary friend. Unfortunately Miss Pyle passed through instead, and was duly splashed. The next day I had to make innumerable journeys with the self-same soap-dish, from the ground floor up three flights of stairs, with water to fill the enamel jug standing in the wash basin!' This was called 'The Punishment Fitting the Crime!'

Connie writes, 'Fun — yes, more often than not involving mischief and breaking rules like playing up after lights out in the dormitories with scrambles into bed, or rolling oneself up in a long curtain, not realizing that bare feet were visible, or diving into a convenient wardrobe to be ignominiously pulled out by the teacher doing last rounds.'

'I remember taking the cross bars out of a girl's bed and

gently laying the mattress on top so when she went to bed she fell through to the floor!' grins a Canadian.

'The poor teachers were distracted in their efforts to teach us to be tidy,' comments an old girl who went to Chefoo in 1892. 'Each night things were picked up and guilty girls had marks taken off. One morning at prayers we saw a table piled high with our belongings. We were told we were to wear these things all day. One by one we went forward to claim what was ours. We went out of the schoolroom wearing pith helmets, carrying books, umbrellas and so forth. Two "missionaries" appeared complete with helmet, umbrella and Bible. "Santa Claus" was carrying almost everything she owned tied to her with string. My notebook became a torment to me as I carried it around in my left hand. By late afternoon we were allowed to shed these belongings, and for almost a week nothing was left around!'

1892. So long ago. But this entertaining little entry in Alan's 1940 diary bridges about half the century, '2nd March: We didn't have our Register Holiday because a dirty rotter stole Johnston's camera!' And, as the century drew to a close in Chefoo School, Malaysia, the ten-year-old girls were queueing up for their dorm aunty to put the finishing touches to their morning hair styles. 'Me first,' sang out a self-seeker, dashing forward with her brush. 'The Bible says "Others first", and I'm the other,' her egocentric friend replied!

Egocentric? Dirty rotters? Horrible brats? Nice people? Angels? Just MKs — the same the century through.

THORN BUSHES HAVE ROSES

Highlighted by the orange blaze ravaging the governor's mansion, the revolutionaries headed across the square, yelling, wielding huge swords and firing guns. The anxious man on the flat roof opposite knew with a sudden and keen premonition who the next intended victims were. The *Yang gwey tse* — the foreign devils of Ningsia. Panic churned somewhere deep inside. Below his wife, with the secret of a fourth pregnancy in her heart, and his three small boys lay asleep. Escape? Was there any hope? The danger pressed nearer as he delayed in his dilemma. Desperately he dashed down from the rooftop, grabbed his three sons from their beds and hustled them with his wife to the back of the little Chinese house. As the family ran barefoot into the night, they heard the mob already smashing windows at the front. So far they had escaped with their lives but all they possessed was left to the looters.

It was November 19th, 1911, and as wet and cold as only N.W. China can get. Chilled by the bleak raw air and trembling with fear, they managed to manoeuvre their way to a church member's home. Dear Nu Li, with the help of a Chinese friend, hid them for three long months.

That added yet another harrowing incident to the jeopardized lives of the little family. The fearsome Boxer Rebellion of 1900 which had wrought havoc with so many CIM expatriates, had caused the mother-to-be of this family to be given up for dead. Yet, unknown to the concerned directors, she and five others were surviving in mountain caves, sleeping in coffins and merely existing on a diet of weeds. The Boxers found three of that group with fatal results but 'mother' came through and 'father' just happened to be one of the reception group who went up the Yangtse River to meet them at Hangkow. No wonder he loved her. She could have been safely pursuing her nursing career in Australia, but because of her concern for the Chinese without Christ she had left herself open to hardship like this in China's interior.

Now, twelve years, a husband and three boys later, she again found herself in a country gripped by revolution. The Manchu Dynasty had been overthrown and Ningsia, a town of 100,000 people near Mongolia, was in the middle of violent upheaval. It would take them three slow months to make it to the coast in those days of mule, donkey and camel rides plus boat caravans down the Yellow River. Yet there was nothing else for it. The monarchy had collapsed and one minor result was that this family was hounded out of the interior — hidden, except to imagination, lies what lurks behind the words. Eventually they reached Hankow . . . Shanghai . . . and finally Chefoo.

Chefoo. Here was asylum at last. The overwrought

Mule travel

parents breathed freely again as they relinquished their three sons (aged eight, six and three) to the care of the Mission School, and there, their fourth little boy was born.

What would happen next? Circumstances in inland China were dire. It seemed sensible to return there with only the baby. So in 1912, with hearts full of thankfulness for the provision for their older boys, the parents set off on their weary way back. And the littlest of the three, now only four, was also left with his two brothers at boarding school. He was the youngest ever to enrol there. It was the last he would see of his parents for five long years. He was nine when they stopped by at Chefoo en route for furlough. They did not take him with them.

'Talk about parental irresponsibility! These persons should never have children, knowing their activities would take them into the more inaccessible parts of China,' exploded one contributor about a similar experience. 'My overall impressions of Chefoo are those of homesickness, loneliness and constriction — the trauma of separation from families was devastating. Whatever we gained academically was certainly lost psychologically.'

'The only childhood I knew,' wrote another Chefusian, 'the only home I had was Chefoo for twelve long years — long, lonely desperate years kept hidden behind my masked face. I kept step with the bells, the teachers, the religion and the social laws of my peers. I conformed and survived. I was a nobody and felt that nobody knew whether I was alive or dead and nobody cared. There was a strange man thousands of miles away — my father . . .'

'I feel,' writes a continental girl, 'as though I was sacrificed on the altar of my parents' missionary career.'

'I hold practically all the blame on my parents,' an Australian adds. 'They deserted me at an age when I needed them. In other words the school existed because parents wanted it to exist.'

'But even then I appreciated what my parents were doing for God,' interrupts an American.

'I've always considered my Chefoo years an advantage — something I'm grateful to my parents for,' a different American continues. 'I suspect I received more benefit than if I had stayed with my parents and had been able to attend some school as a day student.'

'Nothing, I think,' interposes a British writer, 'can really make up for one's own parents, and I always felt sad that I knew mine so little.'

'But,' says another, 'there are parents and parents.'

'And I feel,' interjects yet another, 'that the deprivation was often to such a degree as to be crippling for life.'

Crippling? Hazel's mother had died of typhus. Her father tried to spend as much time as possible with his little daughter during the school holidays, even arranging that others should go on missionary trips in his place. However, when Hazel had already been at home for two months, circumstances arose which caused her father to leave; first he made all the arrangements for his daughter's return to school. At that time, with the government in West China beginning to break down, there were long delays in mail. News only gradually filtered through that Hazel wasn't well and was confined to bed; the trouble was not specified.

It wasn't until father and daughter were reunited that he discovered to his horror that Hazel couldn't walk. Some improvement had been noticed after she knew she would be seeing him again soon and there was nothing organically wrong. Strength slowly returned to her legs during the succeeding weeks as they first flew to Calcutta and then journeyed to Australia by sea. Hazel was walking normally by the time the voyage ended.

'Nonetheless with her only sister in a Japanese internment camp at Weihsien on the other side of China,' writes her father, 'Hazel must have felt very keenly her "aloneness" after I left though outwardly she tried to be brave and look happy. The distress hidden away in her heart finally came out physically in the temporary loss of power in her legs.'

The opinion and experience of some. Yet Hazel's father added a brief but rather telling PS to his letter: 'Hazel, hale and hearty and married to a farmer, now has three children of her own.'

Throughout the years there's always been a long queue to join the PS's, buts and ifs.

'Personality detrimentally affected? My goodness — no!' exclaimed an American who had experienced Chefoo in the 1920s. 'If anyone's personality was detrimentally affected, I'd say it was *his* fault not that of Chefoo.'

'My wish is,' writes another, 'that there were a school like Chefoo in the USA! I have no regrets at all.'

'I always loved school from the time I began until I left Chefoo in 1926.'

'Chefoo influences were tremendous in my life. I'll never be grateful enough.'

'Three things sum up *my* memories,' yet another student from the US contributes. 'Loneliness, homesickness and institutional life. And this was alleviated not at all by any reaching out on the part of the teachers, who were always distant, authoritarian figures. I can remember some teachers only with horror — one in particular bordered on the sadistic.'

'I have tremedous impressions of the *love* of all the Staff.'

'I remember', writes an old girl from the second decade of the twentieth century, 'one very noisy and thundery night with the lightning flashing all round the bay, when Miss McCarthy, realizing that little girls could well be frightened, came round the dormitories and said that if we were scared we could pop into bed with our next-door bed-mate.'

And from England comes the remark, 'Chefoo staff were excellent as "deputy" parents and homemakers.'

'I personally was appalled at the time,' a Canadian ventures to intervene, 'at the way people who might give lengthy devotional talks seemed to take great delight in threatening and caning little boys, whose parents were thousands of miles away.'

'I remember one occasion,' adds an Englishman, 'when about twelve, being involved with two senior boys who raided a tuck shop and took a bar of chocolate each — which we thought a huge joke, just like you read about in school stories. We got a caning which was richly deserved but the episode was blown up out of all proportion and we were held up before the school as 'thieves' and 'sinners'. We were made to sit down and write a letter confessing our sins

The Girls' School dining room

to our parents, which, of course, worried them and made us feel lower than a snake's tummy. I was expected to say I had sinned grievously. This episode was held against me all my school career.'

Was the Girls' School the same? Australia replies, 'We were much too strictly put on our conscience and the slightest little misdemeanour or childish prank was considered a heinous crime for which we were in serious disgrace. We were given Minor Offence marks for the least little thing and Order Marks by the Wardrobe Mistress. After three Order Marks in a week, we had to darn stockings on Saturday afternoons and as a large hole was cut in an old stocking and we were given rough wool, it sometimes took us all afternoon. I remember seeing a large hole in the wardrobe mistress's heel while she was distributing Order Marks right and left for small holes or ladders in our black cotton stockings!

'And each week a teacher brought up the question as to who spilt ink on the stairs, begged the sinner to confess and always ended with a dreadful talk about consciences being "seared with a hot iron".' How that particular issue ended was never quite clear but it was said that they'd discovered the ink splashes were the fault of a Chinese servant.

A member of staff, convinced that May had done something wrong, told her she would be kept in solitary on bread and water until she confessed. After some twelve or more hours ('it may have been 24,' inserts the contributor) May decided it was better to confess to something she had *not* done than go on suffering.

And the Prep? It has been reported to be 'really a rather dreadful school from the living and discipline point of view'. One mistress's leadership is described as a 'reign of terror'. 'Why, for instance, did one little fellow not own up to eating an orange in bed? With great and ridiculous pride it was revealed that the Head found out by finding his handkerchief smelling of orange in the laundry. The miscreant was publicly caned in front of the whole school for this great misdemeanour. Too many times fear and punishment and what really must be considered cruelty were used instead of love and kindness.'

'Right,' concedes an Englishman who experienced Chefoo Boys' School before the Second World War. 'Punishment — we got it — but it was administered with a good attitude. It was rough but I never resented it. It was good to be told, "You take your punishment like a man!" I remember on one occasion our whole class deserved a whack for something. The master in charge straddled two rows of desks with one leg. We filed down a second aisle, had to duck under his leg and feel the bamboo smack against our posteriors as we did so. There were those wily ones among us as speedy as a rocket. With amazing velocity they dodged under the threatening leg and never felt the cane. They weren't recalled to take their medicine. The master had a sense of humour and declared they'd deserved to escape!'

'I remember the teachers mostly for the punishment they inflicted,' adds an American, 'but not with bitterness as they were only trying to keep us little monsters in check — no easy task even then. Night time was the time for shenanigans and how we did have them. Pillowfights and short-sheeted beds were the usual order followed by a story or two before we all quieted down. I suppose depending upon the availability of the teacher we got caught either at the end or the beginning — or maybe even in the middle of the usual nightly activity. One night after the noise had quieted down someone was telling about her experience in the hospital — appendicitis, I think. In marched the mistress in charge with her strap. We all got it and you know I didn't mind because we were all in it together and I was part of the pain. Some were yanked out of their sleep but how was she to know who was and who wasn't sleeping in such a situation? It's difficult to express my feelings. They are mixed when one says "Chefoo". Sadness, tenderness, loneliness, elation, tranquility, order. All these mean Chefoo to me. Now I wouldn't have missed that period of my life for anything in this world. It has helped to make me the person I am today and I am grateful.'

'I consider the system to be monstrous,' is the bald statement of one, now grown, who has nightmare memories.

Chefoo School was a unique project — but was it not able to cope? Was there a dividing line snaking like a skipping rope among the children, separating the popular, sporty extroverts from the shy introverts who, as Dr James Dobson* says, had neither 'beauty: the gold coin of human worth' or 'intelligence: the silver coin of human worth'.

'For the strong,' one past pupil thinks, 'Chefoo was a fine, happy experience; for the weak, it could be a devastating experience from which many took years to recover.'

Why discuss it anyway? Why dig up these unsavoury truths? Why be this honest? Because God was thoroughly honest with us when He wrote the Bible! The seamy side of

* *Hide or Seek* (Power Books, Fleming H. Revell)

many a biblical character, even a choice king like David, isn't hidden.

'There was nothing saccharine about Chefoo,' writes an old staff-member, again unfeignedly. ' "Ascetic" or "astringent" would be truer words. Saccharine could not have produced (a) the really important nationally successful people Chefoo has done or (b) the reasonably successful ordinary happy people with that vein of Chefoo iron in their character.'

'Iron in their character' — like whom?

Although his floggings were not intended to be in direct proportion to his brilliance, nor was he a Chefusian, it is noteworthy to read Winston Churchill's remarks on school in *My Early Life*.*

'I have already described the dreaded apparition in my world of "The Governess". But now a much worse peril began to threaten. I was to go to school. I was now seven years old, and I was what grown-up people in their off-hand way called "a troublesome boy." It appeared that I was to go away from home for many weeks at a stretch in order to do lessons under masters. The term had already begun, but still I should have to stay seven weeks before I could come home for Christmas. Although much that I had heard about school had made a distinctly disagreeable impression on my mind, an impression, I may add, thoroughly borne out by the actual experience, I was also excited and agitated by this great change in my life. I thought in spite of the lessons, it would be fun living with so many other boys and that we should make friends together and have great adventures. Also, I was told that "school days were the happiest time in one's life." Several grown-up people added that in their day, when they were young, schools were very rough: there was bullying, they didn't get enough to eat, they had "to break the ice pitchers" each morning (a thing I have never seen done in my life). But now it was all changed. School life nowadays was one long treat. All the boys enjoyed it. Some of my cousins who were a little older had been quite sorry — I was

* reproduced by permission of the Hamlyn Publishing Group Ltd from *My Early Life* by W.S. Churchill (originally published by Odhams).

told — to come home for the holidays. Cross-examined, the cousins did not confirm this, they only grinned. Anyhow I was perfectly helpless. Irresistible tides drew me swiftly forward. I was no more consulted about leaving home than I had been about coming into the world . . .

'Flogging with the birch in accordance with the Eton fashion was a great feature in St James' School curriculum. But I am sure no Eton boy, and certainly no Harrow boy of my day, ever received such a cruel flogging as this Headmaster was accustomed to inflict upon the little boys who were in his care and power. They exceeded in severity anything that would be tolerated in any of the Reformatories under the Home Office. My reading in later life has supplied me with some possible explanations of his temperament. Two or three times a month the whole school was marshalled in the Library, and one or more delinquents were haled off to an adjoining apartment by the two head boys, and there flogged until they bled freely, while the rest sat quaking, listening to their screams. This form of correction was strongly reinforced by frequent religious services of a somewhat High Church character in the chapel.

'How I hated this school, and what a life of anxiety I lived there for more than two years.'

'Iron in their character' — like C.S. Lewis?

From a chapter entitled 'Concentration Camp' in his delightful *Surprised by Joy** this giant of our time writes about what his school was like:

'The school, as I first knew it, consisted of some eight or nine boarders and about as many day-boys. Organized games, except for endless rounders in the flinty playground, had long been moribund and were finally abandoned not very long after my arrival. There was no bathing except one's weekly bath in the bathroom. I was already doing Latin exercises (as taught by my mother) when I went there in 1908, and I was still doing Latin exercises when I left there in 1910; I had never got in sight of a Roman author. The only stimulating element in the teaching consisted of a few well-used canes which hung on

* C.S. Lewis (Fontana Books; Harcourt Brace Jovanovich Inc in USA).

the green iron chimney-piece of the single schoolroom. The teaching staff consisted of the headmaster and proprietor (we called him Oldie) . . .

'I have known Oldie enter the schoolroom after breakfast, cast his eyes round, and remark, "Oh, there you are, Rees, you horrid boy. If I'm not too tired I shall give you a good drubbing this afternoon." He was not angry, nor was he joking. He was a big, bearded man with full lips like an Assyrian king on a monument, immensely strong, physically dirty. Everyone talks of sadism nowadays but I question whether his cruelty had any erotic element in it. I half divined then, and seem to see clearly now, what all his whipping-boys had in common. They were the boys who fell below a certain social status, the boys with vulgar accents. Poor P — dear, honest, hard-working, friendly, healthily pious P — was flogged incessantly, I now think, for one offence only; he was the son of a dentist. I have seen Oldie make a child bend down at one end of the schoolroom and then take a run of the room's length at each stroke; but P was the trained sufferer of countless thrashings and no sound escaped him until, towards the end of the torture, there came a noise quite unlike a human utterance. That peculiar croaking or rattling cry, that, and the grey faces of all the other boys, and their deathlike stillness, are among the memories I could willingly dispense with.'

These extracts paint a picture of schooling in England in the late 19th and early 20th Century. Chefoo School in Shantung Province, N.W. China was modelled on the English Public School. In those earlier years, teacher training and the understanding of children were very little developed. As a consequence discipline was stern. The term 'child psychology' with all its trimmings and new methods was barely born.

In short, the school was a product of its times. It involved teaching by human beings. And human beings make mistakes.

'Looking back,' admits one of the students, 'I now realize that too many of the teachers were themselves inhibited and so unable to demonstrate the kind of love necessary for the children under their care. The teachers in the Lower

School were all women, most of whom were psychologically unprepared to deal with the mission field and children. All but one, I recall, were spinsters, who now I feel suffered unresolved conflicts of personality and should never have been accepted as candidates. There were too many misfits among them.'

'There was a well-intentioned strict disciplinary feeling about, and applied without favouritism, generally speaking,' contines another, 'but as is inevitable there were some of the staff, and I am writing of the 1910-20 period, who were never intended to care for children. They had been press-ganged into the job by the desperate shortage of staff. The unpredictable behaviour of a few of these contributed to an unevenness of atmosphere. Biblical truth was the permeating ingredient and the Bible the standard of conduct, but personal interpretation sometimes led towards "isolation out from" rather than "separation from" "the world". Standards for worldliness at that time were in keeping with much evangelicalism, far too negative.'

'My brother and I came to Chefoo in 1921: the place which was to be our home for the next ten years,' writes an English old boy. 'The preparatory school was possibly the least satisfactory of the three schools at that time. It was staffed with well-intentioned but not always well-qualified spinsters; its teaching and disciplinary methods were antiquated though undeniably thorough. The atmosphere was strongly religious but too often with the harshness of Puritanism, not with the sunny warmth of essential Christianity. There was too much of "institutional" existence and far too little of the "family" life so obviously desirable for children who were, many of them, virtually orphaned by distance.'

One veteran Chefusian says, 'It is easy to be critical in retrospect. A system of "Family" groupings perhaps in a series of "Homes" presided over by well-chosen foster parents might have been better. But this is no doubt too modern a concept for the 1920s.'

Another comment from England sums up, 'One episode in particular makes me realize that the staff were not always "in touch" — seven prefects were demoted at once for the sin of a book of film stars' photos in their sitting room.'

'We're not perfect,' agrees a once-upon-a-time staff-member, '. . . parents . . . staff . . . children, so we are not immune to possible effects, but I do feel the tendency for a good many years has been always to blame the fact that children have been separated from their parents if anything goes wrong, whereas if we look around, how many cases can we see of those who have grown up at home, in their own homes, who have just as many difficulties?'

One veteran Chefusian says, 'It is easy to be critical in retrospect. A system of "Family" groupings perhaps in a series of "Homes" presided over by well-chosen foster parents might have been better. But this is no doubt too modern a concept for the 1920s.'

A Canadian has something like this to say too, 'I'm concerned that children here at home with their parents all the time are often greater problems and with deeper rebellions than our MKs have ever been — and who's to say that the MKs would have been any better had they remained with their parents in their teenage years?'

In those days the point that it may have been a critical issue for a missionary to send his child away to boarding school was seldom raised. One very ancient reference to the subject did, perhaps surprisingly, occur in a *China's Millions* magazine as far back as 1881 — the year the CIM school began. The title is reminiscent of much that appears in our current Christian periodicals a hundred years later — 'Ought Missionaries to Leave their Children?' The paper enunciates all the reasons we know for parents to care for their own offspring and then the writer pertinently asks, 'Are there no exceptions?' Then, as now, the missionary mother would find the answer in Mark 10.29-30:

'Jesus said, "Truly I say to you, there is no one who has left house or brothers or sisters or mother or father or children or lands for my sake and for the gospel, who will not receive a hundredfold now in this time, houses and brothers and sisters and mothers and

111

children and lands, with persecutions, and in the age to come, eternal life."

"Or children" falters the mother.

"Or children, for My sake," replies the loving Saviour.'

'Having been an MK myself and also the parent of a child sent to Chefoo School I can say it was infinitely harder to send my child to school than it was to be sent,' confesses a mother from Canada. 'But I was so grateful for the time my son was in Chefoo — they did wonders for him and he loved it. When he came home for the winter holidays he asked, "When do I go home again?" — meaning back to school!!! We were shocked for the moment, but then thanked God that he was so happy there and felt at home in school.'

In a letter postmarked The Philippines came this unusual comment 'I feel that we remained closer as a family because we were separated so often. Surely being away from home will not cause a healthy well-loved child to be detrimentally affected. This issue is so hard to answer for we do not know what that affected child would have done in the homeland living with mom and dad.'

The reason for separation — tribal children who need the Gospel

'I know a woman,' interposes a second Canadian, 'who left the Mission to save her child from Chefoo and — the child is a misfit if ever there was one.'

'Physical separation cannot destroy the real unity of a family,' states a different Canadian. 'In fact I feel it sometimes enhances real unity.'

'What we lose in quantity where time is concerned, we gain in the quality of our times together,' agrees an English mum.

'Because we girls,' adds a mother whose own little boy is now at Chefoo, 'knew from the beginning that Mother and Dad were doing what God wanted them to do, we could accept their absence from us. They helped us to understand that we had an important part in their ministry, if we on our part lived to please Jesus at home. We never felt that they were off "doing their thing" while we were doing ours. We knew that it was our family responsibility to carry out God's will together. Each of us now, with families of our own, just continues in the same pattern.'

'Many business people's children are in similar circumstances,' another English contributor puts in a reminder, 'with no prayer and less care in holidays.'

'Meeting many young people in this country, I see there are so many who have much more reason for bitterness,' she continues, 'because of broken homes or parents too busy to bother with them or fathers seldom at home because of pressure of business or mothers out at work.'

An 'old girl' from Scotland gives this slant to the controversy. 'My husband who knows a thing or two about horticulture, says that plants started in a greenhouse thrive better in the open than those that are not. Interesting point. Makes you think just how much the "hot house" atmosphere of Chefoo has helped us to grow up strong and true in this wide, wide world.'

From England, a doctor writes, 'Regarding the deprivation issue, you have got the fascinating question of taking into account the will. We are spiritual as well as instinctive creatures. One of the masters at the Boys' School wrote in my autograph book two lines which galled me at the time but which have impressed my life more than all my other autograph collection:—

"Our wills are ours, we know not how,
Our wills are ours to make them Thine"'

'I feel my personality *was* affected detrimentally,' another past pupil follows on, 'but — deep and lasting spiritual experience compensated.'

In the same vein the next continues, 'For years after coming to Australia I was conscious of the deprivation but eventually came to terms with it and certainly have no regrets now.'

'I feel this is something not to be treated lightly. It leaves scars,' writes a younger Chefusian. 'In my own experience, scars are still there, wounds still healing.'

'Yes, there was a sense of loneliness and homesickness at times,' writes a former student from the Cameron Highlands' Chefoo, 'but one of my fellow school mates was used in leading me to the Lord. She told me that just because I was at Chefoo, and came from a Christian home did not mean I was a Christian. What a great day that was back in 1957. Even though I have had my ups and downs since then, I pinpoint my day of conversion to that point of time. So you see I've always had a special spot in my heart for those school days and even now I regard them as some of the happiest days in my life. No doubt there were times when we hated the place and wanted to go away, but the ony thing that really has stayed in my mind over these years has been the happy times we had together and just what our "Parents" there, at the school, did for us so as to make us feel at home.'

Just how does this dialogue sort itself out in the end? Henry Luce (former editor and owner of TIME magazine) who as an American MK attended Chefoo, was heard to remark, 'I loved it and I hated it.' How true a paradox — Chefoo wasn't perfect but . . .

Thank you, Heavenly Father, for these 'Buts'.

As part of the preparation for this book, hundreds of questionnaires were circulated throughout the world to ex-pupils, staff members and parents. Over 200 letters or completed questionaires were received, the bulk of them

Scale :	very poor 1	poor 2	average 3	good 4	excellent 5	

Box gives average rating for each country:

	U.K.	U.S.A.	Tan.	Aust.	N.Z.
Chefoo preparation for further education in home country	4.3	4.5	4.2	3.7	4.3
Chefoo preparation for life in home country	2.8	3.0	3.0	3.0	2.8
How did Chefoo cope with separation ?	4.3	3.7	4.5	3.9	4.3

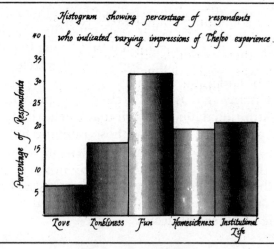

Histogram showing percentage of respondents who indicated varying impressions of Chefoo experience.

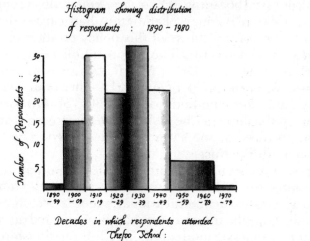

Histogram showing distribution of respondents : 1890 – 1980

Decades in which respondents attended Chefoo School:

from those who had spent most of their school life at Chefoo, and although this was not a properly validated sample survey, these did help to give a picture which described something of the feelings of the people who passed through the school. Asked to comment on impressions of Chefoo from a given list, the 130 who returned questionnaires most often highlighted fun stories and fun experiences as predominant in their thinking. The warmth of love wasn't lacking, but registered lower.

Respondents also felt that Chefoo had given them a fine education (at one time said to be 'the best school east of Suez') but had coped less well in preparing them for life in the homeland. Many Chefusians felt that trying to pick up the threads of life on returning home was like 'treading on thin ice and often falling through.'

In spite of many criticisms of lack of love, punishments and stern institutional life, most felt that Chefoo had coped well with separation. A third of those replying felt some personalities had been detrimentally affected, while two-thirds knew of none harmed in this way.

How do these results support the well-publicized statements that missionary children are the most unbalanced and neurotic of all social groups?

They don't.

Attitudes to boarding school are widely divergent and the Overseas Missionary Fellowship had earlier decided that a survey of the effects of this policy on their children would be very valuable. The Medical Officer at International Headquarters, Dr M.M. Hogben, was responsible for this, with the help of Mr C.H. Sherlock, a survey statistician. The methods and results of this original survey, published in the *OMF Bulletin*, are remarkably similar to those of the survey just described. They were summarized like this:—

'The survey would indicate the following broad picture concerning the MKs involved: they were well-educated and appreciate their educational preparation; they are basically happily married (or happily adjusted to single life); they feel less confident about adult relationships and

116

about their job. The incidence of emotional problems is low among single males and married females, higher among single females and married males but overall probably normal or below normal when compared with society at large.'

So we can understand a contributor's feelings when she writes, 'The balance comes down heavily on the side of the Mission School. It was fun because God was in it and turned all the bitter waters sweet by injecting the Cross of Christ.'

Others add:—

'As far as I am concerned, I am abidingly and tremendously thankful for my Chefoo experience.'

'I have always felt it was a great privilege to have been educated in such a fine school as Chefoo. We had an excellent basic foundation I loved Singing Class and still remember both words and tune of "May Dew" after sixty years!'

This lady went to Chefoo just as the twentieth century was dawning. She remembers, 'When the boarders were getting ready to leave to go home at the end of term, they would auction off any of the treasures in the desks they wanted to get rid of. The owner would hold up the article and call, "Quiz?" and the girl who shouted "Ego" first got it. So as to be sure the auctioneer would not change her mind, one had to add, "No backs!" and it was hers for keeps.

'The name Chefoo always makes my heart "skip a beat".'

'I loved the nine and a half years in Chefoo as a pupil. I wasn't good most of the time but I enjoyed life there and think the training was the best!!'

'With some homesickness, the occasional discomforts (eg chilblains!) and restrictions of institutional life, most of my memories of Chefoo are of the fun we had . . .'

'I was happy there, don't remember feeling lonely (except when I was in trouble), accepted the rather strict discipline as normal, and also accepted the rather spartan conditions as normal too.'

'The Chefoo atmosphere was a bit prim and traditional

but we always felt the staff cared about us and MKs gain more than they lose.'

'As I look back and as I felt at the time, it was the best ten years of my life! Things were started at Chefoo that carried over into later life. I joined the choir at twelve there and have been singing in choirs and community choral groups ever since including one in Los Angeles and in Stuttgart, Germany. Boarding school was a great preparation for Army life. Then there was the hiking over the hills — I still do that whenever possible — and the academic training helped me to breeze through a one-year American High School course (which I probably could have skipped) and my first year of college.'

'One of the most interesting years at school was 1938-39 when twenty-two young men came to Chefoo for language studies, being housed in the "San". It wasn't long before they became known as "The Sons of the Prophets" and enlivened the year with competitions and sports, presenting concerts and readings and preaching at services. The group included three former Chefusians — Sid Best, A.J. Broomhall and Arthur Mathews.'

'I enjoyed every year I had at Chefoo School in the Philippines and feel so privileged that I saw parts of the world my friends will never see. I feel my spiritual background was vitally important and God-given.'

'Institutional life? I think it was great. It taught me how to get along with other people . . . It taught us orderliness, cleanliness, how to behave, how to study, how to care for ourselves and our belongings. Most of all it taught us the Bible and all about God and His love for us.'

Finally it's a delight to draw on this contribution with memories nearly one hundred years old.

'I went to Chefoo in 1892. All in all we had a good time at school. We went home at Christmas plump and rosy, with sleeves and skirts too short, of course. The beach and the rocks with their treasures were a joy. Picnics at the Bluff or Lighthouse Island were long remembered. We enjoyed the Sunday afternoon meetings at the Boys' School — I still remember Mr Mudditt's chalk drawings. The thrill of boarding the steamer for winter vacation after watching the smoke over the Bluff was something special. We were glad to go home and — yes, glad to come back for another year at the old school!'

We need an understanding beyond our own to sum up a debate that has been a hot potato like this for one hundred years. One hundred years? Three thousand years! From that time a very similar event is portrayed in Scripture.

She kept her word. She knew what she had to do. Taking the boy with her on the long journey she left him at their destination. (Somehow have we come full circle and arrived back at the beginning of this chapter?) Her mind was made up. A promise was a promise.

The boy was so young. Only recently weaned. Possibly this could mean that the little boy was only three years old. If anything was going to cause talk, this was it. She — who had so wanted this baby — was leaving him with someone else. Surely such a mother would be distraught.

She went into the temple to pray and we murmur 'No wonder'. Yet as we overhear her words we marvel. 'My heart exalts in the Lord; my strength is exalted in the Lord . . .' When she'd finished praising God the Bible bluntly says, 'They returned home to Ramah without Samuel.'

But if Hannah was disturbed then she was given a poise which was greater than grief. A power outside herself controlled her feelings showing the whole venture in perspective.

And the little boy? What of Samuel left at the temple with an old man who couldn't even control his own sons? Samuel had really been left in the Lord's hands. He lived through the negative forces in his life eventually to become a positive force for God. He was to grow up to say, 'Has the Lord as great delight in burnt offerings and sacrifices as in obeying the voice of the Lord? Behold, to obey is better than sacrifice . . .' That had been Hannah's attitude too and both mother and son discovered that, though they could have complained that rose bushes have thorns, instead they rejoiced because thorn bushes have roses.

A PRAYER FOR PREFECTS

Kathryn has a rather special heritage, being one of three generations of Chefusians. Her father and his brothers — the Judd boys — were at Chefoo School right at its birth in 1881. She and her sister followed and later Kathryn taught for a year there herself. Finally her own children went to Chefoo School, Kuling, China.

'A Prayer for Prefects' was in Kathryn's use in 1924 and Miss Fishe who composed it was headmistress before that time. The words are traditional yet fragrant, setting a Christian tone for those with responsible posts at Chefoo:—

A PRAYER FOR PREFECTS   **by E.A. Fishe**

O LORD, Who didst choose from among their fellow disciples twelve, that they might be with Thee and that Thou mightest teach and train them to do a special work for Thee; we pray Thee that Thou wilt teach and train these who have been chosen to bear any kind of authority amongst their fellows in this school.

May they look upon their office as a sacred trust from Thee, of which they must prove worthy, and as a service for Thee which Thou wilt graciously accept. Take from them all fear which might hinder them from rebuking wrong when they see it, and grant that a desire for popularity may never hinder them from doing that duty faithfully. Give them to realise that what they lack in power and grace to make their service effective, they may claim from Thee who hast appointed them to this service.

May they earn the respect of those with whom they have to deal by the example that they set of devotion to duty, and in striving to serve Thee by serving others may their own souls be blessed.

As those who have served their day and generation faithfully pass out from amongst us into the larger world beyond with its wider opportunities of service, do Thou O LORD, we beseech Thee, raise up others to take their places, all these mercies we beg in Thy Holy Name.

AMEN

STRING OF PEARLS

'Scientists agree that a pearl is really the product of pain. The oyster lies in his bed at the bottom of the ocean and is sometimes invaded by a microscopic irritant . . . The tiny irritant is covered over at the point of the wound. When the wound heals it is a pearl . . . Where there are no wounded oysters, there are no pearls.'*

'One Sunday evening,' wrote the late Mrs Frank Parry, remembering the early days of the nineteen hundreds, 'as the girls arrived back at school after attending church in the "Settlement", they were met by an urgent request for a hot-water bottle from the Boys' School where a boy was ill with cholera (they thought). Then followed three nightmare days, as boy after boy was suddenly taken ill and graves were dug in the little cemetery. Medical help came from ships of the US fleet in the harbour. Girls' School teachers took over the classes in the Boys' School, to lessen the tension and fear as one boy after another stumbled out of the schoolroom to go to the sick room. We girls were kept occupied by making wreaths, breaking off only to attend yet another funeral. A CIM couple with three sons at the Boys' School received a wire, "Herbert dead. Frank dying," and replied "Dear Frank, look to Jesus." Frank was given up, and a message was sent to have a grave in readiness for him, next to his brother's. Thirteen boys died by Wednesday, and the thirteenth was buried in the grave prepared for Frank, who later won many athletic honours, and the Challenge Shield a year early. After 39 years of selfless devoted life in the CIM, he was murdered in south west China, after the Communists took over the city of Kunming. There he found a second grave. He was called the "Resurrection Boy", and awaits the Day of Resurrection for all who love the Saviour and look for His coming.'

* from *Reflections* by Selwyn Hughes (Crusade for World Revival).

This tragedy occurred in the midsummer heat. Lack of sufficient ice for refrigeration apparently caused some chicken pies, which must have been infected, to go bad leading to ptomaine poisoning. Saline infusions prescribed by the American Naval doctors saved Frank's life.

Bubonic plague also hit the Port of Chefoo in those early days. 'A ship from Vladivostock' relates JG, 'had a case on board. The ship was quarantined off the Chefoo harbour, near Lighthouse Island. The story was that some seamen asked to be placed ashore on that island. They were given permission and then stole a junk and headed for the mainland. The school was placed on alert for about three weeks.'

'I remember,' writes Olga, 'landing in Shanghai in January 1911 on our way back to school. We were told we had to stay there because there was a terrible plague in Chefoo killing the people by the hundreds, so everyone was banned from entering. We didn't get back to school until May.'

One old girl who had stayed at Chefoo for the holidays can remember the sad sight of covered stretchers being carried past on the highway behind the school. 'We heard the daily toll of deaths,' she says, 'and felt very restricted within our own walls.'

Danger reared its Medusa-like head in other forms too. One threat to the school happened at the height of the Boxer Rising, in 1900. Arrangements were made to evacuate the children and missionaries to the British naval vessels in harbour at the time. 'To us,' says Bob, 'it was a thrilling possibility, which however never materialized, in the goodness of God.'

'I remember the threat of danger we had from the "War Lords" and their local battles,' recalls Marjory. 'Nightly there was the laying of a bundle of clothes (containing raisins and chocolate as well) on bedside lockers, ready to throw out of the windows before rushing down the stairs. The rowers had their rowlocks ready to dash to the waiting boats more than once. But it never reached that point, though we did shelter once or twice during the nights in parts of the building remote from the skirmishes.'

Wars and rumours of wars, plagues, epidemics, and . . . accidents. Who would have thought that a metal object lying in the hills could turn out to be a grenade, dropped by one of the battling Wars Lords? A young Chefusian, a day-scholar living locally with his parents, picked it up. It exploded. The result was fatal. Who would have thought that an arrow shot at a target would pierce a lad's eye? He lost his sight. Perhaps one *could* hazard a guess that one day, some time in the Far East, a Chefusian would be bitten by a poisonous snake. His life lay in the balance for weeks but today — he is alive! Could a little girl be so severely stung by hornets that her face was disfigured for a time? And broken bones? Yes, but the miracle is that stretched across a hundred years the tragedies have been few. The wonder of it, considering the numerous possibilities for accidents, is that they have not been more frequent.

'And what more shall I say? For time would fail to tell of . . . those who through faith . . . escaped the edge of the sword . . . Others were killed with the sword.'*

In the March 1935 issue of *China's Millions* an editorial comment about the children's adventure with the pirates paints a picture of preservation *and* tragedy:

'While we greatly deplore the loss of life and the wounding of the engineer, we were filled with thankfulness to God that the adventure ended without more serious consequences. For more than fifty years these Chefoo Schools have been in existence, and when we recall the numbers of children who have travelled to and from the Schools, and how the Schools have been preserved in peace during civil war and international strife in which China has been involved, we realize how much cause we have to praise God for His protecting Hand. But the young people do not escape all the perils connected with missionary service, for during the Mission's history more than thirty children have suffered a violent death, in most cases at the same time as their parents' martyrdom.'

Through faith — escaped. Through faith — were killed. Both possibilities were seen in the Chefoo travelling experiences, for our faith is not an insurance policy for *this* life.

* Hebrews 11.34, 36 (RSV)

And so, in God's permissive planning, there were tragedies, sorrows, disquiet, worry, wounds. But the missionaries involved and the Chefusians were of the ilk that loved the Lord, speaking often of Him to each other. And Malachi 3.16, 17 has this radiant hope for them: 'He had a Book of Remembrance drawn up in which He recorded the names of those who feared him and loved to think about Him. "They shall be mine," says the Lord of Hosts, "in that day when I make up my jewels."' (Living Bible). Jewels! Pearls, perhaps? 'Where there are no wounded oysters, there are no pearls — for a pearl is the product of pain.'

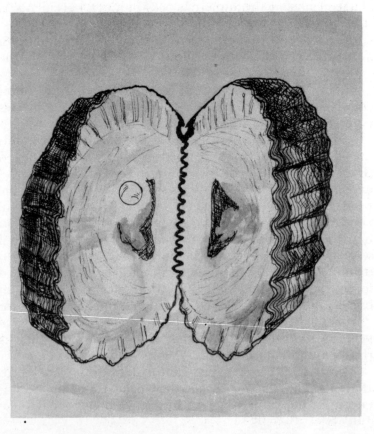

WHEN ICICLES HANG BY THE WALL

'Winter was just setting in and all of us in the boys' school had changed over from khakis to flannels. Cricket and rowing had been over for several weeks, and the choice now was hockey sticks or soccer shoes. The evening of December seventh 1941 found us as usual in the long, stove-heated study hall, bent over algebra books or Latin grammars. Now the time came for us to file out to the chilly bedrooms upstairs. Except for the whispered joke and stifled giggle, there was nothing to keep us from slipping easily off to sleep. Yet for several it was to be the last night of freedom in China and the prologue to an unforgettable Christmas Day.

'We woke to find Japanese soldiers stationed throughout the campus and at each of the gates. Several of the masters were placed in solitary confinement. Gradually it became clear that we were in the midst of real danger, completely cut off from our parents. Hardest of all, no mail came through from the interior. The long winter holidays should have begun in midweek, but now it was quite impossible to travel.

'In the midst of confusion and the loss of anchorage in school and home, insecurity could easily have swept over us like an epidemic. But in God's very gracious provision for us — nearly 400 missionary children — we had teachers who were discerning men and women, who understood the situation and had a godly concern for youngsters not their own. During the next several weeks of uncertainty with tighter security measures surrounding the school grounds, and only the cheerless word of Japanese victories reaching us, the few masters not placed in prison and their wives gave up their usual home life to be especially around, playing games, reading stories, and providing a steady, loving leadership noticeably free from fear. This was undoubtedly the major factor contributing to the general emotional and mental stability of the students.

'But Christmas was due in a little over two weeks. No one could go home, and no presents could be sent to the compound. Even church services were temporarily forbidden. So our boys' school masters came up with a drastic yet deeply impressive solution: each fellow was to give a present to another fellow in his class. However, we could not buy in the shops, and even our shilling-and-sixpence allowances were frozen assets.

'So the day before Christmas the acting headmaster Mr Harris sent every lad to the locker by his bed, where a boy's most precious possessions are stored away. From this jumbled assortment, varying in quantity, each made a selection of his most prized toy or book or pampered gadget, designated it — not necessarily for his best friend — wrapped it as wrinklelessly as he could, and left it in the headmaster's outer office — a spot better known for the unspared rod than for the unspoiled child. Those boys not given anything — unknown except to the teaching staff — were provided for from the faculty homes.

'Christmas dawned, snowy and beautiful. And in the dining room, round the half-grown spruce tree some teacher had hoped to nurse along in front of his cottage for the next several years, the costly little gifts were passed out. It was a very happy time, I remember. Some of us recognized the treasured articles and what they had meant to the chaps who gave them away.

'I said "costly" gifts. But not because they had any great value, except in the hearts of those who gave them. For it is relatively easy to spend for a friend. It was not so easy to tear from its cherished place in our hearts something to which we had become very closely attached. Not a penny was lost to any account; in a sense the celebration cost us nothing, yet it cost us dearly — for it cost everything we had. We knew and could feel painfully that this was not just

128

the giving of a gift, but a giving of ourselves.
"God so loved the world, that He
gave His only Son." '*

*   *   *

Those war years were different, of course, yet ordinarily a handful of children was *always* left at Chefoo for Christmas. Their homes were in remote places such as way up the Hwang Ho and Yangtse Rivers and provinces far inland, which would be impossible to reach in time.

The hardest part of staying turned out to be seeing one's mates pack their cases in a hullabaloo of excitement. The voyagers were taken down to the wharf in rickshaws, bags piled high and waving feverish goodbyes. But once the lucky travellers had gone, it would dawn on the 'stay-ers' that there'd be no more school for two long months! The winter holidays were here and the port of Chefoo beckoned invitingly. They roamed the hills and beaches, rode icefloes with the aid of a pole and, highlight of all, went tobogganing.

'Ye olde toboggan slide,' remembers Stan, 'was situated on a hill which formed part of the caravan route, not far from the school. Amid frenzied yells and whoops the sleds and sleighs would tear down, often overloaded and frequently overturning, occasionally scaring to death half-a-dozen mules or donkeys, who might take to their heels, heehawing in fright and sometimes scattering their loads on the highway amidst the curses and imprecations of their drivers . . . Then back to school for a hot lunch, with rosy cheeks and ravenous appetites, and on to the toboggan slide for more of the same in the afternoon . . .'

Evenings were spent playing games, writing letters home or reading. *Chums* and the *Boys' Own Paper* were avidly digested until the reader become one with the hero of *The Gorilla Hunters* or *The Black Band*. Other literature of an exciting or hair-raising nature was serialized by the master or mistress on duty. Sitting around a glowing fire while the wintry North China winds howled outside, the starry-eyed

*Originally published in IVCF magazine *His*, December 1956.

listeners revelled in *The Hound of the Baskervilles* or *The Speckled Band*. 'I have often thought since,' Stan adds nostalgically, 'that it was due to these long winter evenings at Chefoo that some of us developed our imaginative reasoning and literary qualities which we have found so useful in later life.'

'Perhaps my most colourful memories are of the winter holidays,' Ruth writes, sketching her thoughts vividly. 'Not that I liked winter — I hated it. Chefoo was at its bleakest with icy winds sweeping over a bare landscape, snow and slush, chapped hands and chilblains. But there was another side to it. After we had tried on and then been reissued with our winter clothes, reeking of mothballs, and after the storm windows had been fitted and the stoves installed, we knew that a long two-month holiday lay ahead of us, once the term exams had been hurdled. Boxes and suitcases appeared in the playroom, and packing begun for those who would be going home to their parents for Christmas. We envied them, of course, but the outlook for the handful of 'stayers' was by no means cheerless . . . We played hockey, went sledging or took unwilling trudges, depending on the weather. We were issued with hoggy-doggies — socks (believed to be of dog fur) with the fur inside and worn with "shoes" clearly of pigskin with the bristle side out — all tied to the foot with tape. A more inelegant form of foot gear would be impossible to imagine. I can still see the shocked look of disbelief on the face of a lady in a rickshaw who passed us one day! But they had one supreme virtue. *If* we could get our feet warm before donning these objects (not always possible) they stayed warm even in the snow, and the bristles helped to prevent skidding, which is why they were worn by coolies pushing squealing pigs and other merchandise in heavy barrows along the "Piggy-road".'

'Cold, cold winters' remind another of 'long woolly combinations, flannelette panties and bodice plus serge bloomers topped with sports wool thick blue pullovers, serge tunic and a black cloth overall trimmed with our house colours. Then black woollen stockings . . .

'The breakers froze before they reached the shore and

one terrible year the sea froze solid five miles out. I remember returning from Christmas hols that year, and our ship had to have an ice-cutter going before it to make a channel . . . Each morning before the rising bell a servant would come in and light the fires, giving our drinking water time to thaw before we had to clean our teeth. Our stiff face cloths would cool down the steaming water left at the door to wash our faces.'

Ice — the misery, the cold, the fun of it! The boys found they could walk out at least a mile on the bay, though it was far from smooth. The hunks of ice were two to six feet thick, some standing on edge. Rumour had it that a couple of Chinese drowned when they fell through. After the ice-breakers cleared a channel for ships to get to the harbour, the boys could pole themselves on ice-floes between the shore and the main ice mass. One Christmas holiday, 'a number of us boys went for a walk to The Rocks. Three or four struggled out to Bottle Rock and there hacked out a sheet of ice. They had long bamboos and hoped to push their block to where the ice ended. Suddenly they found their bamboos could not touch bottom and they were floating out to sea! We who were still on the rocks rushed off to a Chinese fisherman who was repairing his nets, and one of us who could speak Chinese asked him to rescue our friends. At last with our help he pushed his boat into the water, and some time later landed the boys on the beach.'

There were the quarries where they could ice-skate ('Weren't supposed to but we did'), the skating rink in the Settlement, and the toboggan run from the Girls' School clear to the end of the playground. The hoggy-doggies did a good job tramping it down ready for the 'zipping down it' to begin. Fun and frolic entangled themselves in the endurance test of waiting for Spring.

As far back as 1886 *China's Millions* carried this picturesque little vignette from one of the Chefoo adults.

'Our beautiful bay is such a glorious sight! How shall I ever describe it! Jack Frost, Father Neptune, and the wind have been having a terrible conflict; the wind has been blowing tremendously, driving the sea hither and thither, which in its turn has seemed to be foaming in fury; it was

The frozen sea

grand yesterday ... to see the white-capped waves far away, and to hear their roar as they came rolling in as far as Jack Frost would allow them, for he in his silent powers had laid hold of the raging sea as it foamed and stilled it with its cold breath and so, for at least one hundred yards out, was a frozen, stormy sea, the waves in some places two yards high, the whole mass as white as snow, because it was the surf that was frozen as it rose and fell.'

Those who stayed at school for Christmas 1935 were treated to this rare event, too — the whole bay became covered with ice that drifted in from further out in the Gulf of Pi-Chi-Li. Another year 'the bay iced clear over to the Bluff. You could take a rickshaw to the ships in the harbour — a pretty solid freeze that year and a different type of scenery.'

Winter! Characteristic of China's north-east coast, it brought its own icy loveliness, its raw temperatures, its misery and fun for the MKs.

With the approach of Christmas, life became really festive. Decorations were hand-made out of red and green paper from which the dye ran madly when wet with paste. They practised carols, stirred puddings and even went on shopping expeditions. 'I can still smell Mr Saito's pungent and overcrowded little shop,' an Australian recalls, 'where it was possible to purchase a few gifts even within our budget. Certainly they needed careful handling, or they might not even survive the trip home.'

As the decorating was in progress, they rehearsed their carols, and by Christmas Eve their repertoire was enormous. Allison remembers their carol-singing expeditions best of all. 'We sang in the piercing cold,' she says, 'by lantern light. It was very romantic but bitter, especially when a blizzard was blowing from the North — and Chefoo faced north! The wind took our breath away as we turned corners and faced the blast. Snow drifts were often deeper than we were tall! We sang at all the houses we knew and often were asked in for a hot drink and for a welcome supper.'

'Christmas Eve was sheer magic,' recalls Ruth. 'We wended our way to the various houses, carrying paper lanterns. Some years snow was falling, sometimes enough lay for us to be glad to emulate the page of Good King Wenceslas and use someone else's footprints, while the coloured lanterns cast a glow on the road. Other years were clear and frosty and the stars almost made a tinkling sound in the frozen sky.'

Despite the late night for the carol singers on Christmas Eve (otherwise unheard of!), everyone was awake early to greet the happy morn. That meant fishing around at the foot of the bed for a bulgy stocking or even, as one male member of the community put it, an early morning pillow-fight. After a special service, it was time to tuck into a wonderful Christmas dinner, followed by games and a present from the huge decorated tree.

'The staff really did all in their power to make Christmas

The Girls' School

memorable for us,' adds Ruth, 'and they succeeded. Nothing that I have experienced since had had quite that atmosphere, and to this day some carols evoke clear memories.'

'I loved the Christmas parties,' a Canadian remembers. She was a Chefusian earlier in the century and also found Christmas merry-making the event of the year. 'I loved helping to make the plum puddings and trying to guess who was playing Santa Claus!'

'I remember Christmas 1913,' says Olga, an old girl from California. 'It was fun. We got up early (us girls) and filled our teachers' stockings that we had somehow swiped from their chests of drawers! Then the boys came up — early, too — and sang carols under our windows. We had fun all day. I thoroughly enjoyed every minute of the two months' holidays.'

The Chefoo Bay spray was still freezing mid-air when January ended and the travelling parties came storming or trickling back, to face freezing dormitories where on bitter nights, the girls took their tooth mugs, filled them with water and placed them on the outside window sills so as to have the dubious pleasure of a mug full of ice to lick in the mornings. Their version of ice lollies!

Back to face warming up an older fellow's bed for him! The shilling-shocker fagging system allowed the seniors to use the little chaps as human hot water bottles and then 'kick' them out into their own cold beds later. No heating of the buildings in those days — just stoves in the classrooms, bedrooms and dining rooms. These, of course, went out and had to be relighted once or twice a day. They did have storm windows facing north, but in the Girls' School, which was up a bit on a hill, the snow blew in the vents under the floors on the north side and up through the floor cracks in the classrooms.

But back they came nevertheless, when the Christmas holidays were over. 'Ecstatic greetings would be exchanged and tall tales told on both sides,' concludes another Canadian. Tall tales — like this one? Mrs Butler affirms this is true.

'Amongst the houses we visited while carol singing on

Christmas Eve,' she recounts, 'was the Rouses'. Mr Arthur Rouse's brother worked for Reiss and Co. You know how Chinese find difficulty in saying "r"? This is fact — one day a man rang up and said, "Is that Lice and Co? May I speak to Mr Louse?" ' — a delightful reminder that though the Christmas celebrations were Western, the setting was that mystic jade land of the East.

The Chinese character for 'Love' — with a few lines added

GOODBYE CHEFOO

'Look over there!'

'Wh-what is it?'

'Snoopers. Grab your baton. After them.'

In the darkness the sixth formers daringly ventured further into the shadows. It was their turn for nightly patrol duty. With Japanese soldiers overrunning the port and starving Chinese continually prowling for food, Chefoo's campus needed watchmen. The grey night duty had suddenly come alive.

Gasping and with batons flying, the patrol bore down on the furtive figures, lurking like spectres behind the garbage bins.

'Hold it! Hold it, you crazy idiots!' Norman and Jack yelled, 'Don't you know friends when you see them?'

Just in time the patrol recognized their classmates, now choking with laughter at the success of their lark.

'Almost too successful,' growled Guy. 'Lucky for you we caught sight of your great white faces! *Very* lucky for you.'

Japan had attacked China in July 1937, and a few months later the invasion, sweeping south, reached Chefoo. One day, as Mr Martin dwelt on the intricacies of the Latin word *castra*, he caught sight of strangers in the playground!

'*Castra* goes like trousers,' he was explaining. 'It is plural in form but singular in meaning. Hallo! Here are our new rulers.'

For several years life continued much as usual. Mr P.A. Bruce, Chefoo's Headmaster, balanced the depressing weight of care with great equilibrium. Despite the pressures of running a school under the miss-nothing eyes of the Japanese, he showed no strain. Then in 1941 'Pearl Harbour' brought the Japanese into World War II and

137

branded Chefusians as enemies. Sentries tramped the compound, food was rationed, armbands had to be worn. Pa Bruce, as he was warmly known, was taken off for interrogation with five other Westerners. Had he not crossed Siberia on his return from furlough and aided political activities en route? Surely he must be a British agent.

Crumpled without him, the staff and children started to pray. 'Lord, was there ever a fairer headmaster, a finer man who knew how to make wise decisions, especially with the enemy guarding our gates? Lord, you know how the children love him, how he understands each boy as an individual, how we can't manage without him . . .'

Several weeks later, four of the men were set free but not Pa Bruce. 'How long, O Lord? Remember, O Lord, what the measure of life is. Remember, O Lord, how Thy servant is scorned.'

'Because he cleaves to me in love, I will deliver him;
I will protect him because he knows my name.
When he calls to me, I will answer him;
I will be with him in troubles,
I will rescue him and honour him . . .'*

The weeks crawled by. School Assembly prayers focused on their headmaster and leader. And then . . . he was free. One day he walked right back into Chefoo life, thinner than before. The sixth man died in prison.

Outside the gate a guard wrote in large Chinese characters on the dusty road, 'I am a Christian — a member of the Salvation Army. Jesus saves.' This was wonderful but, on the whole, the soldiers did just as they liked. Of course Chefoo School's spacious buildings and playing fields, right on the sea front, were highly desirable. It was convenient for them to call in the kitchen at mealtimes and help themselves. Was peanut butter a Japanese delicacy too? Wandering about the houses, they opened doors, putting their names on the rooms they planned to occupy when the Chefusians were forced to leave.

* Psalm 91.14, 15

Was that time right at hand? Furniture was suddenly owned by the Emperor. One guard stuck labels on to say so, while his companion settled himself at a Chefoo piano and played 'Home, Sweet Home'.

The Shinto priests took over the playing field and performed a strange rite, dedicating it to the Emperor too. Bayonet drill on the same field became a common occurrence. One missionary mother, who had rented a holiday house nearby, was appalled to see her four-year-old lying beside them with his pop-gun!

It seemed the beginning of the end.

'It's only a matter of time.' One staff member put everyone's thoughts into words. 'They'll not tolerate the foreigners much longer. What can we do to be ready?'

Each child's belongings were tightly packed into a suitcase but the school equipment posed a problem — the pots and pans, bedding, books . . .?

Then one melancholy day the dreaded word arrived. The Japanese Commanding Officer wanted Chefoo for a military hospital. Forty lorries would be put at their disposal. The move would be across town to Temple Hill. No large building would be waiting there to become a school — just three family-sized houses.

Full of fears and uncertainties, the long crocodile of Chefoo children and staff began to file out of their beautiful compound. There was the Foundation Stone — 'To the Glory of God 1896'. But this was 1942. This was war. It was goodbye to the Science Laboratory, goodbye to the Craft Room, the Art Room, the Library . . . Would they ever see them again?

It was a strange procession. Some, riding in rickshaws, were almost hidden beneath piles of blankets. Everything they owned lay packed into trunks at their feet. Many a long last look settled on the dear old buildings. Surely those running steps didn't mean looters already?

Just then when spirits were lowest, a joyous thing happened. Somebody began to sing the beautiful words of Psalm 46, set to music by one of their teachers, Mr Stanley Houghton!

'God is our refuge,
Our refuge and our strength.
In trouble, in trouble,
A very present help . . .'

Boys with kit, carts and bundles, girls with packages, teddies and treasures, staff with burdens in their hearts passed the fully-armed soldiers and weeping Chinese by-standers, singing — for one after another along the line caught the melody.

And that night as 36 girls tried to bed down in the attic of a house meant for six and now holding 71, they sang the stirring words of

'God is still on the throne
And He will remember His own.
Though trials may press us
And burdens distress us
He never will leave us alone . . .'

It had been November 5th. No guy. No bonfire. But a date the children would always remember. The day they became internees.

'His promise is true,
He will not forget you.
God is still on the throne.'

Was it possible to be a school in a family house? Their headmaster could no longer be with them all. Each house was servantless, overcrowded and lacking in so many things just needed for ordinary living. It was a timeless sort of existence, like being uprooted from a vegetable plot and then left lying on the garden patch.

School work was no go at first — so much time was spent cooking the food and clearing up. But at last, amid all the chores, trunks and boxes became seats for the dining-room cum sitting-room cum classroom cum playroom cum church and even cum kitchen — for at one end a large oilcloth sheet was spread on the floor so that miniature kitchen maids could go to work on the potatoes and carrots when their turn came, like pixies with nimble fingers and large enamel bowls in front of them. And then lessons began, gradually fitting into a short time before dinner and a few hours in the afternoon. Upstairs in the attic, another class got going for the little girls, who sat perched on their mattresses like pilots guiding ships, sailing off into the sea of learning. They discovered that a thimbleful of school procedure could be manoeuvred.

Perhaps cooking was an essential subject in these strange days.

'Do you know how to break an egg?' the teacher asked one boy, who looked particularly clueless about culinary arts.

141

'Yes, sir,' he answered, brightening up and promptly dropped it on the floor!

Did they scoop it up and use it? Food was precious. It had to spin out. Vitamins must be included. Did anyone have better ideas how to feed over two hundred children? Yes, buy some piglets, fatten 'em, kill 'em, cook 'em! A good idea until slaughtering day came around. Miss Carr remembers reading with great volume to the sensitive prep school children in an effort to drown the dying shrieks of their pets!

Each house was visited daily by a very small but dignified Japanese officer and a few of his minions. The 'school' had to line up in a stated order and number off.

'This is how it is done,' he commanded. 'Three days from now, roll call will be in Japanese.'

Consternation greeted this announcement. Just one more drag in the quicksand of war which seemed to suck them further down daily.

Ichi — ni — san — shi — gor . . . impossible in three days, until one master produced a large blackboard and wrote each difficult number down. The school rehearsed and then the board was placed where the students but not the officer could see it. Was that a faint smile almost lighting up his face when they obeyed his orders next time in fluent Japanese? Surprise was there anyway!

But things weren't easy. True, Mr Bruce was given permission to visit the Girls' School under escort. Chats with staff helped. Plans were made. Would these serve for the long years ahead? Could they go on living in such cramped accommodation? Would the children's education be ruined? One subject not neglected was general knowledge. In these long days sheer necessity and inventiveness produced tables, benches, pigsties, chicken runs, a flour mill, water-heating systems and Guide and Scout Headquarters — not to mention *The Temple Hill Tatler*!

Letter were written too — in the hope that even one would get through to worried parents. This one did:

'My dear Mummy and Daddy,

. . . Last Sunday we went to the dining room to sing hymns, we had vilions and one boy came and blue on his trumpet.

It was very nice. We are haveing sesame butter on our bread lots of times . . . On Friday in the night it snowed very hard and in the morning it was very deep. We went out with are guloshers and coats and storm hats and overstockings, we had lovely fun . . . Mr Buzer riecited the village Black Smith and Mrs Buzer played the Moonlight Sonata it was really two cats . . .'

Yet it was almost with a sense of relief they heard the rumour. A move . . . to a really big internment camp where several hundred 'enemy nationals' were already imprisoned. Would there really be more space? Somewhere to play? New things to do? New people to meet?

After ten cramped months on Temple Hill, it was time to pack again.

*   *   *

'Boys — this way.
Girls — in here.
Families — one to each room in that row.
Bachelors — over there.
Loose Women? Right here.'

With an I've-had-it flagging feeling the Chefusians filed in under the most tolerable heading. These tiny rooms? For so many? Swept clean, they boasted only small homemade tables. Again no beds. Nowhere to unpack the contents of their trunks — if they ever arrived. Not even a chair.

Still, it was better than the hold in the steamer or the hard seats in the railway carriage. Better, too, than the cramped quarters in the houses at Temple Hill. So bedding was unrolled, mattresses spread out on a floor once again and gallons of sugarless, milkless tea resorted to. After the dreadful thirst of the journey it was as welcome as rain in the Sahara.

Chefoo was forty-eight hours away by over-crowded boat and waterless train. Yet even that trip had been studded by gems of God's care amid the shale of Japanese inconsideration. More than three hundred were huddled on board the tiny steamer. The staff and children had been squashed in the hold, where they had lain on the boards head to tail. No wonder the packing this time had been so

Chefoo bay

censored by the teachers, and treasures had to be left behind. Would sleep ever come on these boards? How smelly the steamer was and how it rolled, even in the harbour. And the rats . . . But the emptiness inside was worst of all. Hunger. Bread. The baker. Muddled longings turned into restless dreams as the little ship prepared to leave the harbour.

The baker. What had happened to him? All the time they had been at the Temple Hill camp he had brought their bread, and had promised to supply them with loaves for the journey too. He was going to bring them right to the Japanese steamer. Now it seemed he had let them down. Time was short . . . had run out, for the boat hooted a mocking goodbye to the port and steamed off into the bay with its precious load of empty Chefusians. Anxious staff saw the hope of their loaves receding with the shore.

Two nights and a day-long journey lay ahead with no food for over two hundred children. And a blanket of gloom settled over the voyagers, as Chefoo Bay with its dear familiar coastline was becoming merely a backcloth for the drama of life on the little ship. There was the Bluff and Lighthouse Island, the golden beaches, the Bund along which the Chefusians had snaked their way to the church on the hill . . . The old school buildings themselves . . .

But the bread situation was stretching its dilemma over nostalgic thoughts. Right then, as the ship was making its way out of the harbour, another once-upon-a-time story sprang to life to thrill the Chefusians with the joy of knowing God's care.

The Japanese steamer stopped! It anchored in the bay for some reason of its own. At that very minute the Chinese baker arrived on the quay, secured a sampan and sailed right out to the steamer! Skilfully he swung the ambrosia on board, and when the steamer gathered way again all was well.

Oh, the fun to be roused from sleep to taste the crunchy freshness of the new-baked loaves, and somehow to find Chefoo School's favourite chorus encircling their thoughts —

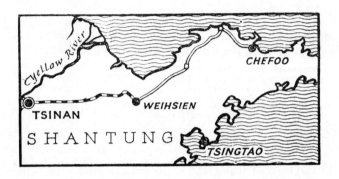

'I have a wealthy Father,
     All the world's gold is His.
Far though the place, and late the hour,
Yet can His simple word of power
     Meet my necessities.
His messengers, from sea to sea,
Wait His command to succour me!'

And now Weihsien Internment Camp — 'Courtyard of the Happy Way', as the Chinese characters over the gateway rather ironically announced. Conditions seemed as packed as ever — one thousand four hundred enemy nationals compressed into what had been the American Presbyterian Mission compound. But one advantage loomed invitingly — the enclosure had a playing field! Imagine. Space — space to run around!

The exciting news that a school had arrived turned the internees into friendly helpers.

'Over here if you need water.'

'I'll show you where we get our meals.'

'I should think we could rustle up a few benches for your things.'

'Put your trunks in the centre when they come. They'll make good chairs.'

'Yes, they'll have to do as tables and desks too.'

'You'll just have to leave everything *in* them.'

And so the empty rooms began to fill up with mattresses, buckets, jugs, baskets, trunks, stores of wood for the stoves that eventually arrived, and meagre rations.

'Hope my turn doesn't come round too often for sweeping the "dorm"!' was a sentiment shared by many. That chore was a nightmare especially in the winter when coal dust settled resolutely on everything. Chores were part of life at Weihsien. The girls washed up millions of plates, the boys pumped oceans of water. The adults, too, each had his job. Everyone needing help thought the Chefusians were the best bet ... fish-cleaners, vegetable peelers, roof-repairers, woodchoppers — the lot. Mr Welch was the bakery manager, producing eight hundred kilos of bread daily (while the yeast lasted). Mrs Welch worked with the vegetable party. An out-of-school job for Miss Carr was making the coal balls from coal dust and a percentage of local clay. She used an old sardine tin for the mixture, and could produce two each time from it. They were then baked in the sun, and petty theft at that stage was quite a grief. Mrs Lack found the laundry another nightmare — four hundred articles every week, washed by the most primitive methods of water and brush (hopefully still with bristles), and soap only sometimes.

Strange how soap could engage one's thoughts so completely. One scouring bar per person per month — for everything.

'No soap left. Chefoo School's short too. They'll pray! More will be here any day!'

If you were under eleven you were too inexperienced to cope with laundry, except to hang it out. How the girls hated that task in winter, when their fingers refused to bend properly with the bitter cold and the sheets turned into frozen grey-white flapping geese before it was time to bring them in.

A staff member might find herself suddenly becoming a tailoress, as happened to Mrs Lack, Mrs Houghton, Miss Williams and Miss Cobb. Surely children shouldn't grow so fast in wartime ... did those boys have their trousers at half mast last week? What a good thing someone thought of dragging down the new dorm curtains before leaving Chefoo — they were just right for summer dresses for the girls!

Food was always of pressing interest. Three large kitchens dealt with anything that came in, even if it was camel

flesh. Milk, eggs and sugar were almost unknown luxuries.
The menu worried the staff:

'Breakfast — millet porridge, black tea, bread

Dinner — curry or stew, black tea, bread

Tea — soup, black tea, bread (and occasionally a sort of
   cake made mostly from the initiative of an enter-
   prising cook)'

Meal Three leaned over heavily on the left-overs from meal
Two where the variety was only the addition of curry
powder.

'Is there any way we can provide the children with
vitamins? I've seen one or two teeth coming through
without enamel!'

'Egg shells have calcium content, you know. That should
help.'

'Really? But how?'

'Save the ones the kitchen put out, grind them down and
administer by the teaspoon . . .'

And so the children had to get used to the powdery,
prophylactic dose as often as it was available. It was a
supplement to the 'hash, mash and splash'.

Birthdays at Chefoo were always special but Internment
Camp celebrations posed a problem. One small girl wondered if just once there could be something different to eat,
for very soon she'd be eleven. And once-upon-a-time, yet
again, a train of donkeys came through the gates carrying
Red Cross parcels! Coffee. Butter. Chocolates. Jam. Sal-
mon. Peaches. Milk Powder and Breakfast Cereal! When
had those last been tasted? So on her birthday morning
Elizabeth found two sweets from one friend, salted nuts
from another and a chocolate heart spiked with currants
made by Kenneth who loved her a lot. If only those
precious Red Cross parcels could always get through, but
with careful rationing this treasure store would last for
some months.

At last summer came again to Weihsien. No coal dust.
No blue fingers. This time — red lumps, and every child
sporting them on arms, legs, torso, all over. That's why
Grace could be seen with her camp bed out in the yard, day
after day for a fortnight:

'I took it out into the sunshine and poured special liquid down all the creases. I mended my mattress. Three times I fumigated it and then I had peace for a few nights.'

Bed-bugs — flat-bodied red one. China's millions! Short of pets, the Chefusians kept them in bottles for observation! On their nightly rounds, the teachers stooped to pick the pests off the sleeping, perspiring children. And if anyone ever had nothing to do, they 'did' a trunk. Everything out, bed-bugs hunted and annihilated, boiling water poured over the empty case, which was then dried in the sun and finally repacked because it remained the wardrobe and treasure chest.

Summer, too, brought Foundation Day. One June 15th was celebrated in a way which was fast becoming a habit. A move! Not outside to freedom . . . a move within the walls of the camp.

The camp wall had shifted into an excited topic of conversation — not because it constantly hemmed them in but because of what happened *over* the wall. The words 'over the wall' held a mysterious ring. Things happened over the wall. Life went on over the wall. Over the wall meant Chinese farmers working on their flat fields. Over the wall held hopeful additions to the meagre diet. Secret bartering was common. Irene's grandmother's wedding ring was worth a few eggs. Gradually the few precious possessions left in the camp disappeared over the wall where the local Chinese were so keen to trade that they risked the death penalty threatened by the Japanese.

At any rate, one day two prisoners escaped over the wall.

'How was it done?' stormed the Japanese.

'Spying!'

'Signalling!'

'From where?'

'Top floor of the tallest building.'

'Evacuate it then.'

'Right sir.'

Now this tall building had once been the American Presbyterian Mission's hospital. It was *the* choice accommodation in the camp.

'Move the children in,' commanded the officer. School-boys would hardly spy or signal.

On 15th June, 1944, the move took only three hours, as just about everybody came to help. Boys on the top floor, girls on the second floor. Why, the whole school was together again! Prayers, roll call, everything would be easier to supervise. And when winter rolled round once more, they had a warmer shelter.

'Clang, clang, clang!' That was the bell for roll call. At nine o'clock one bitterly cold morning the 'hospital' emptied itself for the twice-daily check. Within fifteen minutes the fourteen hundred internees were lined up at the six different stations. Mr Chalkley was Block Warden, hurrying the Chefusians along before the Japanese arrived.

How cold it was. The officer was checking and recheck-ing. Surely he wasn't going to count everybody all over again? But at last the lines could break up. The great thing was to keep warm, for the second bell had not been rung to summon the children into lessons. It was good, too, to keep in practice for camp sports organized by Eric Liddell*, who was an Olympic gold medallist and a Christian loved by everyone.

The girls found an old football. A shot at 'Crack-about' on the tennis court was a good warmer. Among the junior boys was a craze for 'Lungka', and several of them scram-bled round on the ground, flicking marbles into holes. Another had the bright idea of playing leap frog, so most of the boys were either breathlessly leaping from back to back or bending over expectantly as if in Pa's study!

A few managed to find a sheltered corner to read or finish their prep. Several groups discussed the latest camp rumour.

'Have you heard that the Americans have landed at Tsingtao?'

'Watanabi says that our meat supply will be cut by a third.'

Leap frog was changing to a 'fug pile' in a corner. The aim was to get as far in as possible. Groans from the centre, due to the onrush of several hefty seniors, were drowned by

*One of the heroes of the film *Chariots of Fire*

150

the morning bell. Time for work!

And so the drag of roll call twice a day could be a fun experience even in winter. But one evening tragedy hit the camp. It was one of those times when the Japanese took a whole hour to get through the counting.

Five hundred internees waited on the overgrown tennis court — some reading on deck chairs, others laughing and chatting, the Chefoo boys up to pranks.

'I dare you to jump and touch that wire,' one friend challenged Brian.

Brian Thompson was a tall Irish sixteen-year-old, full of fun and games. Touch the wire? Sure he could. It was sagging badly despite repeated requests to the guards to raise it.

Stretching, he curled his fingers right round it. The wire was live. His feet were on the damp ground — shoeless.

With a groan he fell, dragging the filament of death with him. Panic took over. His mother, a member of the school staff, fought the restraining hand which held her back from trying to free her son. Was there *any*thing non-conductive? Yes — the deck chairs! The wooden deck chairs! Desperately men hacked at the wire. At last, Brian fell away. Although doctors fought for his life for hours, he never regained consciousness.

His Christian funeral was a triumph. Pa Bruce reminded the tragedy stricken mourners that while *they* had answered roll call at Weihsien, Brian had responded in Heaven.

'When the roll was called up yonder,
When the roll was called up yonder,
When the roll was called up yonder
He was there.'

Christians. Chefoo School had a reputation for just that, for in the camp the Chefusians were greatly appreciated. In fact in *Memoirs* written by Mr Chilton, the Head Supervisor, he commented, 'Coming from Chefoo as seasoned internees, this group made light of our many labour problems and under their most capable headmaster and his excellent staff, they quickly and cheerfully took over more than their share of the essential camp assignments.' They were known as the 'best organized and most efficient group of all,' and their Christianity rubbed off on Weihsien.

Worldly Weihsien. The whole foreign community of north east China was there — a change from the dreadful segregation of Temple Hill and, let's face it, a variation from Chefoo School where life had always been pretty secluded. Now here was the world, the flesh and the devil — selfishness, dishonesty, broken marriages, juvenile delinquency, undisciplined living, betting, card-playing — the lot.

In addition the Chefusians met new varieties of Christian belief — attractive Roman Catholics and other fine people who didn't really build their lives on the Bible. And the camp's worldliness drew them like a magnet.

It was a shake-up. Weihsien Internment Camp was more 'Christian' than many others and the atmosphere on the whole was healthy, yet it was a far cry from the CIM School. It was the same shaking process that sifted so many on their return home for tertiary education. Chefoo School's sheltered background had long proved a problem for the growing teenager, due to go home.

'It was a traumatic break,' they remember.

'There was a serious gap that couldn't be filled — the ignorance of the boys going from Chefoo into the "wicked world". In spite of the marvellous training at Chefoo, some were knocked over by it. The impact was too sudden.'

'I was terrified of boys when I went home to England. I feel there should have been more mixing of the sexes.'

'Considerable adjustment from "Greenhouse" to "Open Air" was required.'

'The Chefoo School was like a Utopia. Very ideal. But as far as knowing how to meet contemporary life in the U.S. — it was like treading thin ice and often falling through.'

'I was rather naïve.'

'I shall never forget the shock I received at Vancouver where for the first time I saw Europeans performing manual tasks — the unloading of the ship.'

'I felt I was a misfit socially when I came home. I was different, with parents abroad, my accent was odd, clothes strange and I was very shy with an inferiority complex and very bound by convention in order to become accepted.'

'The adjustment to civilization and family life was hard. Our world had had no money, no telephones, no buses, no trains, no shops, no pedigree dogs, no choices, little soap. Some of these were the war and some were the isolation of Chefoo.'

'I was green and made mistakes but . . .'

Weihsien was changing all this. At the time, staff members found it hard to see the school so influenced by earthly standards. But amidst the gloom that sometimes settled on them, they knew many of their protégés were the steadier for the tottering. Afterwards their faith shone, a thing of beauty like the design in a kaleidoscope after the coloured shapes have been shaken together.

'The first five years are worst.' Grace had been staggered to hear this theory propounded by Mr Welch, on arrival.

Five years!

'I'm going to be here forever,' she reasoned. 'Five, ten, fifteen years. I'm going to be old! I'll never go to University. This is very sad. I'll never do anything!'

But a Christian can face this kind of crunch — with God.

'I had a deep consciousness that my heavenly Father was with me and in charge of all that happened,' she wrote later. 'I also had a confidence that no Japanese could touch me unless God allowed it . . . My only fear was that if they won the war they would kill us off first.'

Undoubtedly God was in charge. Mr Bruce actually thought of bringing a pile of Oxford examination papers to Weihsien.

Matric studies in those conditions? Yes — in the boys' dorm. The closely-spaced beds on which the seniors sat were actually mattresses on three cabin trunks. One day heavy boots sounded on the staircase. With great rapidity the lesson on the war situation in Europe was changed to a harmless biology lecture!

And yet during those years of internment, three groups of seniors sat their School Certificate exams. Perhaps the first set had least hope of all. They had tried to study at Temple

CHEFOO IN EXILE

(These lines were written for the Old Chefusians' Party held in the Internment Camp at Weihsien on the 4th May, 1945. They were sung by Mr Houghton to the tune of 'The Meeting of the Waters.' In writing them I had in mind many Reunions of Chefusians far from Chefoo, and I hoped that these verses might someday be sung again.)

On that far-away shore long ago left behind,
How hot was the sand and how keen was the wind,
Where the hills lift their brown rugged line o'er the
Bay
And the junks past the Lighthouse and Bluff glide
away.

The old way of life we've abandoned for good,
With the servants in dozens to answer our nod,
Pirate Bill and Zerubbabel counting the loaves,
And our old Kansampandi to manage the stoves.

What's become of Leander and Hero to-day,
And the Guide Room emblazoned with heraldry gay?
Who to-day use our Field, scene of many a race,
And the Quad., that re-echoed with Prisoners' Base?

"Nihil Absque Labore" 's a true motto still:
God, the Fountain of Wisdom, still shows us His will,
Still upholds those who steadily trust in His truth,
And maturity strengthens the choice of our youth.

SGM

Hill, then after coming to Weihsien had lived for several months hoping for repatriation. Basically they only had six months hard work, and then took the exam at the peak of August's heat. Result? Eleven sat; eleven passed.

Next April fourteen more sat and again all passed.

Neil just missed getting a complete string of A's.

By 1945 rumours of peace began floating over the wall and the one remaining secret radio in the camp caused spirits to soar. The end of the war? Freedom on the horizon? Pa Bruce gathered the Sixth Formers together.

'It's now, or in one or two years after you get home. Take your choice,' he said.

They chose 'now'.

So it was Virgil's and Paul's journeys under a tree as planes dropped food parcels frequently. Would anybody pass?

Pa safely stored the answers. After the war he submitted them personally to Oxford University. Eleven sat that September and all but two passed.

*　　*　　*

'Look! Planes!'

'Those aren't Japanese Zeros!'

'The wings! Look — the markings!'

'The American Air Force!'

'*Friendly* planes . . .'

'It was an incredible experience,' Dr James Hudson Taylor III recalls, excitement quickening his voice even after all these years. 'The sensation was tremendous — to be getting ready for roll call like on any ordinary war-time internment day and then . . . and then a B24!'

The war was over!

The focus of excitement buzzed the campus again making sure it had arrived at its destination. Classes were impossible. The plane dipped its wings twice more — very low, calling almost every internee out of doors to join the wild cheering and shouting.

'We're here, we're here,' they yelled frantically, fearful lest the pilot and crew would not recognize the camp.

The Japanese guards remained on duty at the main gate. What would happen if the crowd rushed them?

Again the plane banked, then swinging over the flat fields of Chinese sorghum outside the camp, dropped seven black dots.

Silence suddenly enveloped the excited crowd. Bombs? Of course not! Not over a field. Look! A canopy was making triangles of each dot. Seven pairs of legs were appearing like the tails of quavers scoring music in the sky.

'Once we saw these parachutes billowing out, we made for the walls,' Dr Taylor continues, 'through the barbed wire which somehow, very fortunately wasn't electrified that day. We didn't trouble to go through the gate. We just tore right out there. The Americans were armed to the hilt. They were expecting to fight it out with the Japanese. Instead they found all the old ladies hugging and kissing them!'

Guards or no guards, over a thousand people thronged through the 'Courtyard of the Happy Way', scrambled over walls, vaulted the wires and swarmed towards the airmen.

Forbidden fields? No! Freedom! The rescuers came tramping through the tall grain, guns at the ready — Major Staeger, two interpreters (one Chinese, one Japanese), a radio expert whose two-way radio came down after him by container, and three officers.

These magnificent angels of deliverance were unceremoniously lifted high by the motley crowd of gaunt internees . . . towards the wall, grey symbol of imprisonment. The camp band was hastily assembling to welcome them. The brass of the Salvation Army suddenly burst forth with a medley of national anthems — a true Victory March which had been practised hopefully over and over again, the melody line carefully absenting itself!

But did the Japanese know that the war was just about over? Had orders come for them to lower their bayonets? Anxiously the head-high heroes watched for any hostile moves. Fifty well-armed Japanese soldiers hesitated as their Commandant struggled with conflicting urges. Was the war truly finished? Should the camp be handed over to a mere seven paratroopers?

Released from his perch just inside the gates, the American major approached the Commandant's office. Silence enveloped the crowd once more — a theatre could not have presented a mime more tense. The possibility of tragedy loomed in each mind, except perhaps in those of the children who were still excitedly coming to terms with the thought of liberty.

Inflexibly the two leaders summed each other up. Then slowly the Japanese samurai passed over his sword and gun.

'Where's my old headmaster?' a young paratrooper called out. 'Is Mr Bruce here?'

Incredibly, among the parachutists was an old Chefoo boy! It was an unforgettable day.

Mr P.A. Bruce, headmaster 1930-1945

'Then five of us boys took off', concludes Dr Taylor laughingly, 'and ran the five miles into Weihsien just for a taste of freedom. We called at the Belgian Roman Catholic Mission where they welcomed us with soft drinks. Incredible! And then, after that regular supplies were dropped by parachute and we older boys used to go to pick them up. Canned tomato soup! Imagine! But it seemed so rich-tasting after our meagre diets, that it made us sick!'

And the liberators settled in the camp and began the process of reorientating the internees. Glossy magazines, blaring radio, food and more clothes dropped from the sky, trips outside the wall and — no more roll calls!

With the reawakening came questions.

'These are photographs of another internment camp? But *we* never actually starved. We weren't brutally man-handled. Hardly anybody died here . . . Few are sick . . .'

Had God arranged for the Commandant of *this* camp to have attended college in the U.S.? Was his mild rule due to memories of a liberal regime in sunny California? To complaints about the hash, mash and splash, he had merely replied 'I beg you to consider the Japanese soldier — he is very happy on four fish cakes a day.'!

'And how come the parachutists arrived on the dot of peace?' Up in the hills, two Chinese guerilla bands had planned to capture the camp. The internees would have made valuable hostages. Yes — a raid on the camp as soon as the peace treaty had been signed . . . But news had filtered through. Had God timed the rescuers to start two hours in advance?

Yet, it had been two and a half long years with food so poor that the American liberators couldn't eat the grand menu cooked up to celebrate their rescue operation — even though it was complete with carefully-hoarded specialities. By 1945 rations had been so meagre that the courses suggesting stew or millet had all been pruned to bread — bread porridge for breakfast, bread pudding for dinner, bread — hard, dry bread — for tea.

With the slump in supplies had come a corresponding droop in spirits. Morale in the camp had sunk to a new low.

People were weary of internment, of hunger, of ragged clothing, of the freezing winter with insufficient fuel, of bed-bugs in summer and of the ever-present colony of rats. They were tired of the cesspools, of the continual labour to keep the camp going, of trying to keep the peace — tired, tired, tired.

But August had arrived. August 1945 and American emancipation. Weihsien was daily sliding into history. The great exodus was about to start. Home. Freedom. And perhaps Chefoo again?

The ruined Boys' School seen from the north and the quad

THOUGHTS ON RUINS

Ruins are a grim reminder of better days
They reveal facts as they are, undistorted. It is true to say of
the accompanying photographs, 'Here are the remains of
the CIM Boys' School', but that is a merely superficial
statement. History has been written in the very stones.
Almost every nook and cranny has been the centre of some
incident, some secret, some escapade.

Yet now nothing but memory and sentiment can linger
to any advantage round the quad, the schoolrooms, the
corridors and the masters' rooms.

Ruins invite constructive thinking
What is God's purpose in allowing the devastation of a
building that for more than forty years served as the home
of the sons of many missionaries? Whilst it was adequate for
earlier days, was it suitable for the modern schoolboy? Did
it lend itself to adaptation as a home after 1934 when the
new classrooms were built for co-education? Emphatically,
no: it was bleak, gloomy, ill-suited as a home for children
who so rarely saw their parents: it was built to house only
half the number of boys who eventually occupied it; the
staff houses at either end had few facilities for convenient
living.

Ruins remind us of past opportunities
Before 1930 a thousand boys had attended the school for
longer or shorter periods; a good percentage of these were
in full-time or part-time service for the Lord, in the mission
field, in the home ministry, in professional business or trade
circles. News is continually reaching the staff of the affec-
tionate regard in which Old Chefusians hold the school.
Many express gratefulness for an education which, despite
its handicaps, tended to a sturdy independence of character

founded on the sound basis of an attitude of reverence for God and eternal realities and a sense of responsibility towards their fellows. The formation of good habits of industry, honesty and dependability has had much to do with the success of many an Old Chefusian. The School was the spiritual birthplace of many down the years.

Ruins may upset a sense of proportion
The Boys' School is only one of many buildings on the CIM Compound at Chefoo. The structure and roofs of all the other buildings still stand, even if the interior of most is completely stripped. Communist soldiers are quartered in these buildings now, and there is a Chinese school making use of the Preparatory School building. Is God our Father grieving over the losses? If not, why should we? Has He no alternative for us? It was God who ordered Cyrus, a heathen king, to rebuild the house of the Lord at Jerusalem: it was God who provided the silver and gold: it was God who, through Darius, gave an order to those who attempted to spoil the work of building, 'And that which they have need of . . . let it be given them day by day without fail.'

Ruins are a call to the prayer of faith
The new temple was not built without careful consideration, planning and expenditure of money and time; neither will the new CIM school be. It is *now* when God is leading us in the dark that we need guidance and patience as well as strong faith. Here are subjects for prayer:

> The site of the future school; the provision of funds for building; the selection of equipment and staff; premises to meet the needs not only of the CIM but of the children of other missions.

Written by Stanley Houghton and published in China's Million, March-April 1947.

CHEFOO NOSTALGIA

What is it?

As a Canadian who has now spent probably the greater part of his life in Canada raising a large family and making many friends over the years, I can recall from time to time meeting and hearing people reminisce about childhood spent here and boyhood spent there, and I cannot ever recall wishing or feeling that I would have preferred to have lived my childhood or boyhood elsewhere than at Chefoo.

Perhaps that is Chefoo Nostalgia. But it is also a great deal more. It covers the Hills — the Baby Towers on register holidays — the J.R.'s and the War Arrows — football cake matches — Tuesday bump supper nights, exeat — winter holidays spent at Chefoo, and the love and kindness that was especially then showered on us who were away from home.

It has also in it summer holidays and my Birthday Anniversary picnic party usually held at Second Beach on August 2nd. It includes Foundation Day, Exhibition Day, Sundays when we could gaze on the particular girl of our choice and dreams, who usually was dressed in white and ribbons and who looked to us as a dream girl.

I do not know what it is about Chefoo but I cannot think of it without happy thoughts and comforting thoughts. I now realize beyond my limited expression of words how much thought and preparation was given and prayer offered up for each one of us who was entirely unaware and ignorant of what lay ahead for us out in the big world beyond Chefoo.

I think of Stooke and the gentle and kind influence he exerted to train us to be Christian gentlemen. I think of McCarthy and his bushy beard and eyebrows, who was so scrupulously impartial and fair. I think of Alty, who was conscientious and yet a character, who could only be

Mr F. McCarthy, headmaster 1895-1930

understood after many years of retrospection. I think of many others; some are still alive today and others have also passed on to their eternal reward.

I think also of my school companions, and I have now hanging in my office a school photograph probably taken in 1918 when I was a Third Former, and which I believe today is as alive as if it were yesterday. Faces suggest names — names suggest anecdotes.

We lived in a sheltered cove. I often wish I could transport my own growing family of five sons and two daughters and have them raised in such an atmosphere of discipline, regulation and good habits so necessary in our daily lives, but yet as I see it now all about us were teachers, matrons and others in charge of us who cared for us with infinite Christian love and patience and human kindness.

May some of those who laboured often so long, so late, and without any apparent appreciation, now be gladdened by this little memory of Chefoo Nostalgia and a late realization that it was not a vain effort.

WASR

(from the CSA magazine, July 1957)

CHEFOO . . .

. . . *in* China but not of China
. . . an environment of well-intentioned kindness
. . . a nostalgia and permanent interest in anything to do with the old place and days
. . . Public School transplanted to the East with vast overdoses of religion
. . . a unique bond, linking all of us, anywhere in the world, of all ages
. . . an isolated and abnormal society — fascinating but not healthy
. . . Miss Dix — a gem of a teacher
. . . dark, slippery, slimy, stone, scorpion-harbouring bath tubs
. . . firm and lasting friendships
. . . eating everything on your plate, even horrid egg plant
. . . the best ten years of my life
. . . shades of Queen Victoria
. . . hoping there'd be cricket in Heaven
. . . losing out on family life
. . . picnics at places with magical names — the Cherry Orchards, the Bamboo Temple, The Bluff . . .

. . . not knowing how to boil a kettle or peel a potato
. . . Mr Murray — his picture hangs on the wall of my study at home
. . . knowing no American history but being able to recite, even now, the counties on the left and right banks of the Thames
. . . an extension of the gentlemen and ladies of the British Empire
. . . being taught *how* to work
. . . better and more relaxed with co-tuition
. . . being trained to keep a daily Quiet Time
. . . no Science Lab. in the early days
. . . the greatness of Pa Bruce
. . . knowing nothing of the land we lived in
. . . good literature and musical appreciation
. . . one big happy family
. . . rough
. . . an austere atmosphere
. . . the wonderful atmosphere of sheer joyful faith, understanding, infinite patience and love of the staff
. . . either passive suffering or active acceptance
. . . for Jesus' sake

BOTH SIDES OF THE HUMP

'Can't fit the children to parachutes,' explained the pilot. 'You wouldn't want to jump without the children! And *we* couldn't jump without *you!*'

No parachutes! No parachutes for *any*body. And they were flying over the Hump — the high dangerous mountains of the Himalayas.

It was Christmas Day 1944, and dusk was falling in West China. The information about parachutes didn't exactly reassure the Chefoo escorts, ushering their charges forward for their first plane ride.

Kiating, thousands of miles inland, had housed a little emergency prep school for children who were cut off from the real Chefoo by the war with the Japanese. Now even the isolation of Kiating in Szechwan wasn't safe.

'Get them out,' came the order. 'Evacuate!'

How? Where?

India was nearest and safest — safe except for the flight over the high intervening mountains, where many a plane came down. American army trucks drove the precious little band to the airport for the first lap of the journey which would take them to Kunming, Yunnan. It helped to sing together just as their school-friends had done when forced to evacuate the real Chefoo,

'I will not be afraid,
I will not be afraid.
I will look upward,
And travel onward
And not be afraid.'

So Christmas Day was spent at the airport. Noon was the scheduled time of the flight, but noon came and went. The army made the delay worthwhile by serving turkey plus all the trimmings on aluminium trays!

Slowly the afternoon dragged by like a wait at the dentist's and then at last the word came: 'Board.' Board an ancient DC3 in pitch black night with no parachutes. The escorts tried to still their own fears. Kunming was having air raid alarms almost every night, and that meant all lights out. How could their plane land in the dark?

The engines started . . . the engines stopped. A flaw was detected, repaired and, as a sort of afterthought, the time was used to load on more fuel.

Again the engine whined, and they were on their way at last — whirring, soaring through the night. It would be a two-hour trip. Mrs Williamson eyed her watch nervously.

'Nearly there?' she enquired an hour and a half of black sky later.

'Another hour or two to go,' the crew member replied vaguely.

Mrs Williamson shifted her position uneasily. The blackness. The uncertainty. The war. The responsibility of all these little ones . . . A second crew-member interrupted her turbulent thoughts.

'Oxygen!' he said.

Oxygen? Yes, for army planes did not have pressurized cabins in those days. The night wore on. Suddenly one of the children collapsed.

'Oxygen!' cried Miss Elliott. 'We need more oxygen.' As she pounded on the cockpit door, it was difficult not to sound hysterical.

'Sorry. It's all used up,' was the reply.

> 'I will not be afraid . . .
> I will look upward . . .'

The teachers prayed. All at once the little door opened again like a ray of hope.

'For two hours we've been lost,' a voice announced, 'but now we're over the Yunnani Airport. We're going down.'

Finally the wheels hit solid earth, and the crew emerged.

'Never again!' exclaimed one.

'Let me get out and kiss terra firma!' said another.

Departure from Kunming for India, 1944 (drawing by Clarence Frencham)

Relief brought a new sense of well-being. Even the collapsed child was fine again at a normal altitude. But the respite was brief. The aircraft was refuelling in preparation for continuing its flight to Kunming.

'I don't want to go in the plane again,' came one little voice, saying what they all felt.

But there was nothing else for it. Back in they piled and this time an uneventful flight landed them at Kunming about 2 a.m. Ham and eggs were served — their first meal since Christmas dinner at noon the previous day.

In a friendly way an air force man came to chat with one of the missionaries. 'You know,' he said, 'our plane landed at that last airport with almost empty fuel tanks.'

The missionary gasped.

'We wouldn't have been able to stay in the air ten minutes longer,' he added. 'I did more praying on that trip than I've ever done in my whole life.'

Journeys in China, especially those connected with Chefoo School, tended to be like that. Lengthy, hazardous, full of delays, of almost not making it, of prayers — constant prayers to a loving Heavenly Father asking Him to keep the children's guardian angels working overtime. Many a heart sank, many an accident almost happened, many an incident was just avoided ... And arrival at Kunming didn't even mean the Hump had been conquered yet. On they went.

Strapped in their uncomfortable little seats lining the sides of the aircraft, the children had to cope with the problem of eating, the problem of passing a pot for toilet facilities, the problem of breathing at such an altitude.

But they made it to Calcutta. There a refugee centre helped the children until arrangements could be made for them to go on to Kalimpong in North East India, only a few miles from Darjeeling. At last government trucks arrived — rather late — to convey them to the railway station. So great was the hurry to board the outgoing train that coolies grabbed all the baggage and rushed towards the carriages with it. Staff and children tried to do likewise. One lad, quicker than the rest, managed to get aboard the train before it started ... *one* boy. One Chefoo boy and all the baggage while the rest of the 'school' looked on in dismay from the platform!

'Fortunately,' wrote one staff member from the vantage point of thirty years later, 'Steve was able to get the train stopped before it got really out of the station. Then we all clambered aboard. It was not exactly first-class travel. As I recall it, there were two freight cars reserved for us. The coolies had thrown the luggage in a pile in each car, and we were to arrange ourselves for an overnight trip as best we could.'

Stories other than fairy tales have good endings. It's nice to know that in this real-life situation, at least the next one and a half years were good for Chefoo scholars in the beautiful foothills of the Himalayas.

* * *

But what was Chefoo School doing there? On 7th July 1937 Japan had attacked China. In December, the invasion sweeping south reached Chefoo, and it became increasingly difficult to cross from Free China to Japanese-occupied China. CIM parents far inland had children due for schooling — what should be done about them? So towards the end of 1940, plans were made to open a little emergency preparatory school in the province of Szechwan, West China, at a grey riverside town called Kiating.

So one evening in late summer 1941, two little boys from Kansu and two young teachers disembarked from a small houseboat and picked their way to rickshaws which took them to their new compound. It was a roundabout journey from the river to the school, for the city had recently been bombed and, in fact, some of the ruins were still smouldering.

'The war will soon be over so we can get along with the minimum of equipment,' was the attitude happily taken as in the autumn of 1941 school opened with ten children and four on the staff.

A parcel containing about a dozen assorted readers, a few exercise books and some sample cards arrived from Chefoo, but that was the extent of their teaching aids, and no more came through. Poor quality pencils, paper and chalk could be obtained locally. Yet in a wonderful way the Lord did keep adding to their little library through gifts from friends, and great was the glee the day a huge box of coloured crayons arrived. Text books were almost unprocurable, though, and the staff carried on the school with its steadily growing little band of Chefusians under great disadvantages.

The supply route to the coast had been closed for some time, so clothes for the children were just about unobtainable. Some Chefusians had complete school outfits left in readiness in Shanghai, but their parents now had to resort to desperate improvisation. Things like buttons, fasteners and elastic were irreplaceable — some little girls had to have the same length of elastic threaded in *each* clean pair of pants! 'My worst memory,' says one old boy sadly, 'was having to wear my sister's dress because we had few clothes. I was of a highly nervous temperament and had a hard time of it.' The hardship of wartime conditions made life at Kiating rather grey, yet Theodore says, 'My memories of Kiating are very happy. It was more like a family than a school.'

Yes, brush strokes of colour highlighted the shade. Once the picture was cow-shaped! The compound boasted an anti-foreign heifer and stories of hasty exits, when the cow exhibited her decided antipathy, peppered life. Though far from amusing then, it causes a chuckle now to recall the time when she broke from her tether and chased a teacher across the garden, head angrily lowered. The children playing on the bank screamed in fright but before anyone could run to the rescue (and any other European would only have enraged the neurotic animal further) the chase ended abruptly as Elizabeth, failing to see a ditch newly dug across the garden, fell into it. The cow pulled up in confusion at her victim's sudden disappearance, enabling the house boy to approach and grab her broken rope.

Three other bright spots warding off the gloom of those years were swing, see-saw and wheelbarrow. The latter was so much in demand that a year later one small Chefusian wrote, 'We used to have a wheelbarrow and now we have a wheel.'

Left to themselves, the children's favourite game was gouging out roads and air-raid shelters in the bank. The obsession with air-raids was rather distressing to the staff, especially as one little girl showed obvious nervous trouble as the result of many raids on her home city. One day Miss Bailey planned a treat for them: an excursion to the river. With cries of joy the children leapt from the boat and, to a man, began to dig air-raid shelters in the sandbank. Gradually, however, air-raid warnings in Kiating decreased in number and, in fact, all the time that the school was there not one bomb was dropped in that city. Enemy planes were frequently heard overhead, though. One night when there was an air-raid alarm, a teacher was checking the rooms for stragglers and found a little girl crouched beside her bed muttering to herself. The teacher moved quickly forward in concern, but the child was only groping in the dark and saying, 'Where'th my other thlipper gone?'

The most colourful highlight of Kiating days was the summer holiday trip to Mount Omei, a cool retreat from the heat. Clarence, who didn't see his mother for three years or his father for five, recalls the jaunts vividly. 'We searched for "crystals" in the cornfields,' he writes, 'small, diamond-bright crystals of quartz. I shall always remember crawling down the rows, the bright sun dancing down thru the corn stalks which grew way above our heads, whilst within an hour or so we collected perhaps a dozen or so of these beautiful little rocks.' Another year he recounts, 'This time we were more daring in our forays into the bush. We came across many snakes and there were all kinds of wild life. I remember seeing a chameleon, and huge multi-coloured dragonflies with a six to eight inch wing-span. This holiday was the first chance I had of swimming in a large pool. It was built on a steep hillside and was filled from a stream. It commanded a beautiful view. The water was kept in with a large wooden plug, but being fed from a mountain stream there was a thick layer of mud on the bottom. I remember one of the teachers lost their glasses in the mud and so they had to pull the plug out and drain the pool. That really excited all the boys as, to empty it, one brave adult would have to dive under the water and pull out the large plug. We all had visions of the poor chap being pulled under by the suction!

'The war was getting closer now. We saw aeroplanes going over. Then one day, when an American light aeroplane crash-landed near the river, we were taken on a special trip to see it. Apparently it was unharmed apart from the propellor, which was damaged. Eventually a new propellor was obtained and the aircraft returned to base. However, the airmen gave us the old one to play with, so for a long time afterwards we would make the shape of an aeroplane out of rocks and stones with the old propellor at the front. We sat on the ground and our imaginations did the rest!'

Back at school, staff dinner was interrupted one night by shrieks from the little boys' dormitory: 'It's a spook! It's a spook!' they cried. 'Our beds are moving up and down.' Lights were switched on. Nothing out of the ordinary seemed to be about and as long as the staff stayed there, all was normal.

'The airmen gave us the old propellor to play with' (drawing by Clarence Frencham)

A few nights later it all happened again. And again after that! Each evening there was a calming-down routine, and nothing unusual could be found in the dorm.

'We came to the conclusion,' recounts Frances, 'that the culprit must be one of them, in fact the newest member of our family, a first grader who had been in school only a few weeks. I was always reluctant to ask a suspected culprit, "Did you do that?" so when I called this lad into the office I said, "Alan, how did you lift those beds?" "Like this," he replied promptly, crouching down and then jerking his head up suddenly! "We don't do things like that in school," I assured him solemnly!'

The second year at Kiating saw the number of children increase to thirty, putting an even heavier strain on resources. Other problems cropped up too. Some of the new beds which had been made for the children proved to be inhabited by bed-bugs. Making the rounds one night, a staff member found one boy literally crawling with bugs. There was only one thing to do. Swaying with sleep, he was made to stand on an oilcloth sheet, stripped and brushed down from head to toe, while another teacher hurled bedding, mosquito net and clothing from the balcony.

On a different occasion, the children were complaining in the morning that they could not find small articles of clothing, earnestly denying the charge of carelessness. Then a sock was found outside a window, caught under a tile . . . leading to the discovery of a colony of rats!

'That second year closed with an epidemic of measles among the children,' recounts Ruth, 'and a matrimonial epidemic among the staff — both of serious proportions!' One little girl remembers being one of only three who didn't catch measles, and how that little trio sat on the front doorstep fervently wishing to be feverish, as the staff were all busy looking after the sick.

Three and a half years rolled by. Kiating school now had an almost complete change of staff and the number of children had multiplied again. And the war was getting closer. Because of the sudden sweep of Japanese armies inland, consular and mission authorities decided to get those for whom they were responsible out of menaced areas as quickly as possible. So late in December 1944 41 CIM children and part of the staff left Kiating for India, on that dangerous journey 'over the Hump'.

*　　*　　*

Kalimpong. What did this roof-of-the-world location hold for the Chefusians? Years later one little girl described her time there as 'Open air life interrupted by lessons!' Annette was asked to join the staff and describes her journey to the foot of the Himalayas, with artistic words that wing the beauty home.

'A normal-sized railway train took this new recruit north from Calcutta. From that she had to change on to a narrow gauge railway with a wee toy engine right out of a nursery book. She proceeded puff puff up the valley with the mountain rising steeply on the one side and falling on the other side, down to where the pale green river flowed — a river that had come all the way from the melted snows of the Himalayas. Higher and higher she went till the little train finally stopped and she transferred herself and her baggage to a waiting taxi. And then what a ride! Up and up, round and round, sometimes passing over by bridge the road that had just been traversed below.

'Then finally she arrived at the town of Kalimpong, a market town for Tibetan wool and a meeting place for Indians, Tibetans, Sherpas, Nepalis, Bhutanese and others. Not far from here the expeditions start off for their journey to climb Mount Everest, and right here one has a magnificent view of Kanchenjunga, the third highest mountain in the world.'

Miss Frances Williamson, who was principal then, wrote for *China's Millions* in 1947, 'We couldn't always see the mighty range of snow-capped peaks that bars the way from India to Tibet — no, that was not a sight which grew commonplace by being daily before our eyes: it was reserved for special times, when the air had unwonted clearness. Then a short walk to the top of the hill would be rewarded by a scene that left us hushed and breathless as we worshipped in awed silence the Creator of such grandeur and loveliness. And though we could not always see the snows, we lived daily with the beauty of the hills about us, and praised God for the works of His hands.'

At night they could see the lights of Darjeeling, 'like diamonds' says Annette, 'flung down on a piece of black velvet, twinkling and glittering in the rarefied air. And lying in bed at night we could hear the howling of a jackal close at hand, as he visited the dustbins looking for a snack.'

The children of Chefoo School Kalimpong, aged from six to twelve, ran barefoot between the classrooms and the dorms, on the grassy slopes of the mountain. They were delighted that their shoes wore out all too quickly in the rainy season and it was hard to replace them! This beautiful environment was ideal for nature study. One night a jackal was caught in a trap and Mr Carlburg shot it. The animal became the visual aid for an anatomy lesson. Afterwards the remains were placed out on the cliff edge and gigantic Himalayan vultures gathered for a feast. So sated did they become that they could scarcely rise to fly off and could only get airborne by waddling to the cliff-edge and taking off from there!

'Birthdays were an occasion for a party,' says Annette, 'and everyone gave a present, perhaps an original work of art or a treasure sacrificed from one's locker. But why the drawing of a grave with a cross on it for one member of staff? A necklace for Mr Carlburg? "Well, he can give it to his wife, can't he?" said the little girl whose gift was being called in question!'

Was discipline a problem, with so much open-air life? 'I remember the spanking room,' laughs one old girl ruefully. 'We had black marks for every conceivable thing and so — repeated spankings over a trunk with a belt on the rear end. A weekly performance for me!'

All the same, the emergency principal was ingenious in her efforts to improve discipline. Facing an epidemic of children asking to be excused during lessons, she offered a reward to those who managed to overcome this bad habit. But some parents were mystified to receive the following news in a home letter: 'Miss Williamson gives us sweets if we last all week without going to the toilet!'

At last the time came to leave Kalimpong, after just over a year there. The war was over. VJ Day had been celebrated by a huge bonfire. Some left their beds early to see, for the last time, the sun rise on Kanchenjunga, its snowy peaks turning from deep rose pink to gold to dazzling white.

After an adventurous journey to the humid heat of the plains, a coastal vessel was found to take the children and staff to Shanghai. Another Ruth takes us out of the forties and bridges the gap to the eighties with this little memoir: 'The ocean voyage took a month, and school met daily on the deck. Fresh water was in very short supply, and each staff member used a pint carefully to sponge bath each child in her cabin daily. The ship was a freighter and had no facilities for swimming or showering.

'It was July 4th when we dropped anchor in Singapore harbour. The question was whether to continue school or try to find a way to get ashore for the day. One girl at the rail said sadly, "Why do we have to have school today? I'm half American!" '

But the little Chefusian need not have worried, for a way was found to go ashore, and the trip to Singapore Botanic Gardens was a highlight of that twelve-hour holiday.

'Little did we dream,' says Ruth, 'that some day Overseas Missionary Fellowship headquarters would be right across the road . . .'

THE FALL OF THE BAMBOO CURTAIN

Kuling, Central China. 1951. Spring. Another exodus . . .

"'Why are you in China?"

"Because my parents are missionaries here."

"Why are they missionaries?"

"Because — well — because they felt the call of God."

Up and down went the sing-song Mandarin-speaking voice of my interrogator. Why was he asking me these obvious, simple questions?

Through the open window pungent odours of steamed rice and quick-frying cabbage wafted up from the street below.

"What do missionaries do in China?"

"They preach and teach the people."

"What do they teach?"

I did my best to summarize the essence of Christianity. Not far away I could hear the harshly-sweet voices of children singing their newest song:

> "Mao ts'eh tong, Si-ta-lin,
> T'ai yang tsai tien kong chao."
> (Mao Tse-tung, Stalin,
> Suns in the sky, shedding light.)

On my left the interpreter — a plump missionary with a sweet face and bravely floral dress — translated questions and answers with quiet efficiency. To the right a scribe covered page after page with skilful brushstrokes. What could there possibly be in my answers worth such assiduous recording!

"What do you learn in school?"

"English, History, Scripture, French, Maths, Chinese History . . ."

"Ah, Chinese History! What do you learn about that?"

It was a subject I enjoyed, so I expanded enthusiastically, until the poor man was positively wriggling with impatience.

How unexpected life was! A few weeks ago I had been just another schoolgirl in Chefoo School in Kuling, Central China. Today I was being interviewed as though I were a spy, by a Communist official with a poker face and khaki voice . . .

"What do you think of the war in Korea?"

My mind snapped to attention, aware of the missionary-interpreter's warning glance. We had been briefed about this kind of question.

What did I think of the war in Korea? I thought it was monstrous, senseless, wicked . . .

"I don't know enough about it to give an opinion," I said primly, sensing the interpreter's relief and the official's disappointment.

"Where have you been in China?"

"Tachu, Tahsien, Shanghai, Chungking. I can't remember every place."

"You must not answer in this way. Where else have you been?"

"But I tell you, I can't remember. I was only a baby some of the time."

"Have you been to Omei?"

"Oh! yes, I have."

"Then why did you not say so?"

When it was over and we were in the street, I turned to the missionary.

"How did he know all those things about me?"

She explained that the teachers had had to prepare detailed dossiers on every child in the school.

"Then why do they question us?"

"Because, my dear," she said, "they cannot believe that the school is what we say it is — a boarding school for missionaries' children. They believe the premises are a front for imperialism and that all missionaries, willingly or unwillingly, are agents of imperialism."

180

"What is this 'imperialism'?" I asked.

She smiled.

"Most of *them* don't know the answer to that question. All they know is that it is one of the things they must strike down."

I was suddenly afraid and indignant for my mother and father in their remote corner of Western China. How could anyone believe them to be imperialist agents? What would happen to them?

Arriving at the school gates, all other considerations shelved, I revelled in the unaccustomed limelight which my interview had brought me. Friends ran to greet me with cries of:

"What was it like?" "Did they hurt you?" "Lucky you. I hope I'm the next. It's so exciting!"

Excitement — that was the feeling uppermost in our childish minds in the early weeks following those few shots heard at midnight which had heralded the Communist takeover of our beautiful hill resort. To us, the ensuing days seemed like a page out of an adventure story, a game, little more. We knew that we and our parents would be asked to leave the country, so assumed that in no time at all parents and children would be reunited and flown to their home countries. Meanwhile we settled down to enjoy our real-life drama.

We couldn't take the soldiers of the liberation army seriously at first, as they marched solemnly round the premises on surprise inspections.

"No one will tear up paper till next inspection," they announced after one visit and we were highly amused as the days passed to watch the piles of scrap paper growing taller and taller. The fact that none of the officials could read English didn't seem to worry them at all.

As yet we were still free to go for walks to Dragon's Tooth, Hyke's Valley or Little Elephant. Best of all were the early morning "bird walks" bringing occasional glimpses of the golden oriole, winking like a jewel through the feathery bamboos, or that flash of blue lightning which heralds the presence of the compact-bodied and elusive kingfisher.

Gradually our feelings of excitement changed to uneasiness and then to fear. Children threw stones at our approach and shouted "imperialist" — to them a term of unparalleled abuse. Rumours of "liquidations", "indoctrinations" and "purges" — though we scarcely understood the implications — worried us.

Early in January, 1951, we had been told to pack up and leave within a few days. But weeks of packing and unpacking, order and counter-order had followed and not until February 28th did the first party receive final permission to leave. My brother and I went with the second party on March 16th.

"Ninety-one, ninety-two, ninety-three . . ." Our party was engaged in counting the "Thousand Steps" which constituted the only route down from our mountain paradise. I made it — as I recall — nine hundred and ninety nine, amid scenery which looked as though it had been luxuriating undisturbed since the beginning of time. The only other travellers were some coolies carrying their sedan chairs up the hill.

In the village we settled ourselves as comfortably as possible into a decrepit truck. A few seconds before "take-off" a group of Chinese men seemed to spring out of the ground and swarm onto our vehicle. No amount of persuasion or argument would induce them to move, so there wasn't even standing room left as we bumped our way along rutted tracks.

And so began our journey to the Bamboo Border; a journey fraught with worry and weariness, yet set against the unforgettable background of a Chinese spring — the last spring I should ever see in this land where I had been born and brought up. Waterlogged rice fields, edged with the purple and fragrant bean-flower, looked for all the world like new-laid lawns. In a few weeks men and women would be standing knee-deep in mud, thinning out and transplanting the crop. On higher ground yellow-gold mustard-seed flowers made dazzling carpets. Here and there we saw cherry and almond trees heavy with blossom. Riding through this peaceful loveliness, one found it hard

182

to believe that the country was in the aftermath of a military revolution.

Not so in the towns. There the evidences of "liberation" were everywhere: in the monumental posters of Mao Tse-tung and the slanderous anti-Western slogans and pictures on walls and hoardings; in the revolutionary songs and the hostility we met; in the confident bearing of the officials and the cowed servility of the people.

On March 22nd we reached the emotive border between Red China and British Hong Kong. A sad straggle of schoolchildren and teachers, we joined the long queue and inched slowly forward. We had been told not to show our feelings, but our weariness made the injunction unneces-sary. All I longed to do was to sit down.

And then an astonishing thing happened. No sooner had the group immediately in front of me crossed the "line" than a transfiguration occurred. Blank-faced men and women were laughing or weeping for joy. I saw big men rushing forward to kiss the flagpole of the Union Jack. Such emotion was infectious. I, too, experienced a sense of release as I stepped into the free world.'

*   *   *

Crossing the border

183

And so the students and staff of Chefoo School, like Jean, left China — for good. Now, not only the port of Chefoo was left behind but also the great land itself, along whose coast the much-loved port lay. Their final resting-place on the mainland of China was the old army huts in Kowloon. Was the school a thing of the past too — a memory only of pre-Communist CIM days?

And Kuling? Where was that?After the war didn't they go from Weihsien Internment Camp back to the real Chefoo — the real Chefoo School which had grown from the deck timbers of a wrecked ship to a village-sized campus?

In 1947 the top men in CIM could see that a return to the original Chefoo was becoming less and less likely. The premises had been spoiled by the Japanese. Even before they ever reached Internment Camp the staff had witnessed beds and desks being flung out of top windows. The compound there had catered for three hundred children; now numbers had tumbled to one hundred. Remoteness was also a problem, because Chefoo was only easily accessible by ship and big companies like Butterfield and Swire were still not operating after the war. Chefoo School, Chefoo, Shantung Province, China was in the past. The remaining nucleus of children was operating in the mission headquarters itself in Shanghai, having just arrived from India. The long-suffering staff there was coping with the hundred-plus children who had swallowed up the General Director's sanctum and had even over-flowed into the very Council Room.

That's when somebody mentioned a smaller American School property on a mountain, 450 miles up river where the slopes rose steeply from the Yangtse plain.

'Too inaccessible,' was the comment of many but — one glimpse of this mountain heaven convinced the scouts that it was *the* ideal location for the new Chefoo School.

Throughout the years at various stages and for different reasons the CIM school had had little off-shoots or subdivisions in Tongshin, Kuling (in early days), Kiating, Weihsien Internment Camp, Kalimpong at the foot of the

Himalayas in India, and straight after the war in the CIM Shanghai Headquarters. Yet they were one — one school which began to take the name with them. It was Chefoo School now, whether in the Port of Chefoo, China or not. Uprooted from the original Chefoo, pupils and staff were eager that the name should go with them. And the governors agreed.

Fortunately for everyone the school's stay in Shanghai was only temporary, for those who went to spy out the land brought back tremendous reports of Kuling. The pros and cons were listed: how could they get supplies for a whole school in? was it wise to settle so far from the coast? However, it did seem that the Lord was leading that way. An advance party went ahead, but despite all their preparations the first group of children arrived while they were still using candles!

One great reality which sealed the choice of location as the Lord's, was the peppercorn rent asked by the generous American Mission — US $1 per anum!

'From the first, Kuling appealed to the young people,' runs an article in *China's Millions* at that time. '. . . the freedom of the hills, the lure of mountain streams, the wealth of flowers, the rare moths and beetles, the haunts of birds, the exquisite beauty of frozen mist on tree or shrub, the glow of sunset behind dark mountains . . .'

The names of nooks or picnic paths spelt enchantment — The Cave of the Immortals, The Temple of the Heavenly Pool, the White Deer Grotto, The Temple in the Clouds, The Three Waterfalls — they conjured up tales of fantasy, spiced by the setting in that Eastern land.

Even on a bleak day, Kuling breathed 'such stuff as dreams are made on'. Thick drifting mist would swirl round the school just as today 'The White Witch' eddies around the buildings in the Cameron Highlands, Malaysia. To the nature-lover the cloudy veil couldn't hide minute miracles like the dripping ice sheath on each pine-needle sword. On the school's special pine they could be drawn off like gloves, and the branches tinkled like the ping of finger nails on crystal when the wind from the overcast sky stirred them in the night.

Kuling heights

Winter's beauty was breath-taking. A well-chosen name
for the hotel-turned-holiday-home for CIM parents was
'The Fairy Glen'. Snowflakes and frost together turned the
wiry bushes into a fairyland of lacy ice doilies with their
petrified spiders' webs. Tobogganing down the long school
drive, shooting off a ramp and cascading on to the snowy
playing pitch below was one of winter's joys. In fact, snow
suits were part of every Chefoo child's outfit list!

Early spring meant wild azaleas on the hillside. Then came roses, tigerlilies, jasmine, gentian, edelweiss and enormous scented violets. Every type of tree lent itself to climbing, fern gardens asked to be created, huge rock pools beckoned the swimmers and abandoned houses lured the trekkers. A favourite haunt was one which was commandeered by a local man for his pig. Super fun to stalk the animal!

Two of the staff were enjoying the rewarding relaxation of birdwatching as they sat one day on old grey stone steps. A white butterfly hovered, the earth and wet leaves smelt good. A wind rustled the bamboo. The call of the bird, the tickle of the butterfly on a hand, the clouds drifting over 'Land's End' in the distance, the tapering purple-black downy bamboo — all gave a perspective to life, seeming to seal in the joy of serving the Lord in this beautiful spot He had chosen for His school.

In summer, too, the cicadas were grinding their chorus in the trees, sounding like numerous bicycles fed with air from squeaky pumps, and their caps released to let the gas hiss out again. From early morning till dusk the unremitting syringes were busy and in winter the hills seemed strangely silent without them.

On an autumn day in 1950 the children from one class went for a nature ramble to the Three Trees. Later that evening when all the little ones were tucked in bed, the teacher stopped by her classroom, strangely silent at that hour of night. There she found their little piles of leaves ready for pressing. Alistair's sou'wester lay on his desk, and Margaret picked it up to find it hid a treasure trove of coloured jewels — shiny wet red leaves, shiny golden leaves, shiny curled brown leaves — all shapes and sizes. Amongst them lay the glistening dark green needles of mountain pine, and on the pines was a hairy caterpillar! Later in the season, that same teacher mounted a small nut-coloured leaf on the corner of her diary page. 'Little Philip pushed this tiny leaf into my hand,' she wrote. '"Would you like this little leaf? It's a sort of moon shape."' This was a particularly emotive entry because little Philip

Chefoo School at Kuling

met with an accident on his return to the UK on furlough and is in heaven now.

How they rejoiced in their surroundings. What thanksgiving was returned to the Lord for His creation, for His protection on the long journeys to reach that mountain idyll, for the presence of His angels watching over little ones all day long. The following spring, Margaret's diary unfolds this little bit of carefree Chefoo life. 'We went out for a long walk to Dragon's Tooth yesterday afternoon . . . dry, crackling brown and yellow grass and undergrowth beside the path, rustling dry bamboos, shrivelled fluttering leaves, scrunchy snow under your feet, slush and mud, mud, then clean white snow again under dark pine trees, a file of men with straw sandals and loads of wood out carrying. Poles, snow-covered tea bushes in a little plantation . . . Averil scrambling on to a rock — the tooth of the dragon itself — and nearly scaring me out of my wits because of the drop of hundreds of feet sheer below, and the knowledge that if the child behind her should sneeze that would be the last we'd see of Avy this side of Glory.' No one sneezed and Avy's angel brought her safely back to Chefoo! Since those days the Lord has taken her to Thailand and now her own two little girls with their brother go to Chefoo School, Malaysia.

The Kuling Chefusians had a certain amount of pocket money each, and a real treat was a shopping spree when little trinkets were bought for family or friends. The teachers taught the children how to set aside a tithe and floated various projects which the pupils actually financed. One day in 1950 the school notice board suddenly sported a unique photograph — Averil's father on a Tibetan pony. Her sister, Linnet, captured the snapshot in words, 'He was wearing a thick sheepskin gown and boots and a leather hat with flaps over the ears. I can see that photo up on the school notice board to this day. I was so proud of him!' The children had had a share in buying that much-needed horse for treks into Tibet. Suggestions for a name flowed in to Mr Martin who chose two Chinese characters pronounced *Bow-she*, meaning to announce joy or happiness. So the name was a very good one for a pony to carry a missionary up hill and down dale. The Tibetans congratulated the new owner of *Bow-she* by presenting scarves to tie in his mane.

One thrilling Sunday President and Madame Chiang Kai-shek came to worship in the little church the school used. They sat in front and the fascinated Chefusians behind stared wonderingly at the president's shaved head! Madame was one of the most elegant ladies they'd ever met. And meet they did, for after church the awed children, every one of them, were shaken by the hand.

Can it ever rain in the mountains of the Far East! One day in a really heavy downpour, the compound manager was clearing debris out of a drain when his dentures fell out and were swept away in the flood! A calamity of the blackest in inland China. The whole school was mobilized to hunt for the teeth, but although the Lord was besought by many a small intercessor there was no sign of them. It so happened that one teacher wrote of the loss in a letter home to her mother — a conscience-smitten mother who had ordered a new set of false teeth for herself when her old ones were still perfectly good. 'This must be of the Lord,' she thought, and with all haste she posted her teeth — the new ones — to the school. Yes, you've guessed it — they were a perfect fit for the compound manager!

Ted and Margaret were houseparents for the junior boys in those days. 'They were as happy as any years of our life,' Ted recalls. 'We thrived under the happy leadership of Mr Stanley Houghton. How friendly and varied the staff was. I have been teaching for over twenty years in Australia since we left and I have not seen such concerted care by staff for students who found things difficult or unhappy. The united staff prayer meeting was a telling factor in our lives.' The time at Kuling saw his first happy experience working with Americans, and he speaks appreciatively of the ladies on the staff as 'capable and consistent . . . the wonderfully sympathetic guide mistress . . . beautiful people.'

The opinion of a staff member. And this is what a Kuling Chefusian thought, 'We loved our teachers and staff members. I suppose they must have had some time to themselves, but my impression is that they gave themselves to us at all times. Mr Martin was a special favourite. He loved the Greek classics and used to read such wonders as the Odyssey to us by the hour — translating from Greek as he went.'

*   *   *

Not even a bicycle could be used for transport at Kuling. The approach to the beautiful mountain resort culminated in the thousand steps which rose ever upwards on the edge of a precipice so steep that the headmaster, Mr Stanley Houghton, used to stand at one perilous bend as though on guard till every Chefusian in the party had climbed by. Yet not only the students made it successfully to their home in the clouds but also such impossible items as pianos, a generator, sports equipment, tools, books, stationery,

clothing, food and even — cows! To the children that last-named bulky milk-laden 'parcel' was the most appreciated. The safe arrival of Buttercup and Daisy had been eagerly prayed for and the building of a cowshed supervised by very young foremen with much enthusiasm. What joy when the first calf was born, the fascinated beholders learning the facts of life as a reluctant placenta was coaxed away by tying an old shoe to the cord! Yes — the cowshed was a much-loved spot frequented day after day by the same animal-lovers.

One tragic day in mid 1950, Mr Houghton walked all the way down the mountain, escorting a group who were returning to their home countries. On his return, he opted for a quick game of tennis without pausing to rest, and he collapsed on the court.

Hurriedly he was carried past the children to the doctor's house. The campus was transformed from a noisy happy Shangri-la to a tense and hushed waiting room. Supper time came and went without the team there knowing what they ate. And then it was evening assembly hour. Instead of the well-known figure of their head, Mr Martin climbed to the platform. The atmosphere was so solemn and still that

most of the children realized, even before they were told, that their headmaster had gone home to the Lord.

Amid sobbing and with quavering voices, the leaderless school sang the lovely words that Mr Houghton had himself composed

'Oh praise ye the Lord for His leading
For He leads by the way that is right.
Before us He goes and behind us
He protects us with mercy and might.
By the strength of His arm there is quiet
Till His saints are passed over to rest.
Oh praise ye the Lord for His leading
For He leads by the way that is best.'

Mr Stanley Houghton, headmaster 1946-1950

Never had his music been so moving, although he had delighted the staff and children over and over again with his compositions. His great musical gift had been used to write the melodies for many songs, to move the school by his beautiful piano playing, to train the choir for first-class performances and to join Mrs Crapuchettes in duets. Under his leadership, music had played an important part in the school curriculum. In fact, at one stage they had so many teachers with musical gifts that out of 133 children a hundred were taking piano lessons.

It was the end of an era. At a time when the Communists were beginning to take control in the mountains, a time when tension around was mounting, Chefoo School was left leaderless.

And the funeral? One little girl of that time remembers, 'We walked up the hill to the foreigners' cemetery. We knew it so well. It was a favourite destination for weekend walks with the more imaginative ones among us memorizing tombstone data and concocting the most heart-stopping stories. It was the only other place in Kuling where English could be read. And so it was a friendly place for our beloved Mr Houghton to be laid to rest, especially as we knew he was alive with the Lord.'

Mr Houghton had loved children so much. It was he who had written this little snippet for *China's Millions* when the school was still in Shanghai — showing more than accounts about him ever can, his deep concern for and joy in young folks:—

'The children are wonderfully friendly and there is a very happy atmosphere in the school. The boys live on one floor, the girls another. Next term we shall expand into another building, as we expect twenty new children, mostly of six years of age. The staff is united and we are very conscious of the Lord's presence. We had an uproarious welcome, but the crowning touch was when I opened a card of welcome handpainted with the text, "My son, if sinners entice thee, consent thou not." Two or three six- and seven-year-olds pilot me down the corridors holding my hand, and I even unexpectedly received a kiss from a youngster who sprang into my arms! One has to be prepared for anything! . . . It certainly is a tremendous responsibility to bring up other people's children. Pray that some young men and women may hear the call to this grand work.'

And he had been prepared for anything — even death.

Years later another, who was a little girl then, wrote, 'There was no one in the school I loved more than Mrs Houghton and she had been more patient with the training of fiery little me than any other staff member. I avoided her after her bereavement until the message was sent to me, "Mrs Houghton is so sad that you are not greeting her!" Mrs Houghton could think of *me* at a time like this? What love filled my heart as I rushed out to make her a little posy of flowers which was tenderly acknowledged. It was this continuously loving relationship between children and staff that colours my memories of Chefoo and makes me so grateful to God that our four children can be educated there too.'

* * *

1950 was a traumatic year for Chefoo School, Kuling. They had lost their popular, beloved principal and also had increasingly to face the threat of Communism creeping steadily closer. The children were cushioned from much of the anxiety and fear of the future which must have tormented the staff. Tension enveloped the school at times just as the swirling mist wrapped the mountain paths in cloudy weather. Little changes were occurring more and more frequently. Teachers and older children were taken off for questioning from time to time. It was forbidden to burn even the tiniest scrap of paper in case, perhaps, the XO XO XO pattern on children's letters was a secret code. Huge crates appeared in the corridors into which went even their sweet papers. Red rice-paper seals made their appearance on cupboard doors, pasted there to claim that the contents now belonged to the People's Republic of China. Nervously the staff kept an eye on them, genuinely concerned lest the more exuberant children would rattle a door and break the flimsy bit of paper.

Radios were forbidden. One staff member kept a wireless bricked up in his wall, so that during the night he could hear the news on short wave and seal up the wall again before morning. One never knew just when the guards would burst in, invading their privacy and keeping everyone on tenterhooks.

Inflation was sweeping across China too in the same way as the Communists were making more and more territory their own. Dollar bills became increasingly numerous and, inevitably, almost worthless. Only one type of currency was stable and worth having — the silver dollar. Where was the school in Kuling, cut off by fighting from Shanghai, to come by such treasure in order to exist?

It was thrilling to watch how the Lord was caring for His little team. One day a lanky missionary from Nanchang came striding into the compound, followed by a coolie carrying dozens of Carnation milk tins. The unwitting carrier never knew what treasure had been slung across his shoulders, for the cans were packed full of hundreds of silver dollars! The missionary had made a marvellous deal with the local merchant who wanted to travel light and was happy to exchange his load for a cheque to be cashed in Hong Kong. The money lasted for the school's needs throughout the Communist rule — a brief factual statement but pregnant with the practical meaning of God's love.

Even in the event of picketing when they could neither get out to buy food nor have merchants bring it in, God had gone before. Mrs Carlburg had happened to buy, at a special low price, extra meat which she had salted down ready for a hundred hungry children. And with the help of such measures as bartering sugar for tea within the staff families, everyone got through, the worst privation being the rationing of bread to one slice per meal.

Obviously the time came when the little band of CIMers could stay no longer, and the school had to be evacuated. They came out in two main groups — a dreadful experience and responsibility for the staff. The mountain march alone was nine miles, plus another six to reach the nearest town on the plains. The smaller children had sedan chairs but older ones had to walk down those thousand precipitous steps in the snow. It was dark when they made it to the nearest inn. Exhausted and footsore, they thought the steaming noodles served there the best they'd ever tasted, which made up somewhat for the feast the bed-bugs had that night.

The journey south began next morning — a seemingly endless train ride when loudspeakers blared out Communist propaganda. On reaching Canton each child had a wide repertoire of red songs flowing in the blood-stream and imprinted so indelibly on the mind that they are remembered to this day. Hauled out at every railway station, they were frisked by guards and their belongings unpacked on filthy platforms for inspection, each time a few more items being confiscated.

But one never-to-be-forgotten day, they, like Jean who

started this Kuling saga, reached the barbed wire barrier separating Communist China from Hong Kong. English soldiers stood with welcoming smiles under a fluttering Union Jack. Their God had worked on their behalf and had brought them to freedom.

A free world. Chefoo School in China was only to be a memory. In the May issue of *China's Millions* that year a heart-tugging little comment ends an article on Kuling:

'It has been left behind. Staff and children are now scattered in their various home countries — North America, Australasia and the British Isles.

"Peace, perfect peace,
   The future all unknown,
Jesus we know
   And He is on the throne."'

YENTAI TODAY

Dr Alfred Crofts, professor of history at the University of Denver and a Chefoo old boy, actually went back in 1972 to the scene of his boyhood days on that coast. He wrote, 'I was one of the first group of Americans invited by the Chinese government to visit the country in recent years . . . and the only one to see Chefoo.

'I arrived in Chefoo in the early morning of a drizzly overcast day . . . From the hotel balcony I looked rather eagerly along the shore towards my boyhood haunts. The beach had disappeared entirely, covered, I was told, by rubble and paved with stones forming an esplanade that fell away to the ocean in an eight-foot sea wall . . . No bathers, boats or playful children would ever use the beach again.'

Chefoo had gone. Yentai was back.

Yentai means 'smoke terrace'. Small mounds on the hills at Chefoo indicated that once smoke signals sent out their warnings when pirates were approaching. Today 'the smoke-stacks of steel mills can be seen, belching yellow fumes.'

Today the Chefoo Schools alumni would find Yentai unfamiliar. The foreign buildings have vanished, 'replaced by barracks, warehouses and an enormous military auditorium. A massive eight-foot wall enclosed the old compound. Landfills erased the gullies and streams . . . The cricket fields had become a military parade and manoeuvre ground,' and the East Beach was sealed off as a military reserve.

'Yentai had destroyed a beach, constructing in its place a long plaza open to the sea breezes, where parades and mass rallies could be held. It was far more difficult, moreover, for an invading enemy to storm a high sea-wall or for saboteurs to climb it, than to land on a beach. Compared with these advantages, what was the value of sailing boats and playing in the sand?'

Another Old Boy who went back to China, as recently as 1979, is Mr David Clark who left Chefoo in 1942. He too visited the old school site but, like Dr Crofts, saw little of the compound, inaccessible as it was to visitors. But one high moment of that nostalgic experience stands out for him — he was able to put his hand on the old boat shed that still stands on the shores of an Eastern Sea.

Chefoo had faced outwards — geared to life by the Pacific. Yentai is orientated towards Asia — sending produce and manufactured goods to the inland West. 'A microcosm of the New China', Dr Crofts called it. A complex of new 15-metre boulevards replaces the mule traffic tracks and the routes for caravans of camels seen at the beginning of the century. Focus was shifted from the harbour to industry . . . 'metal goods, textiles, cigarettes, diesel engines, canned fish and fertilizer are produced and shipped to inland China.' Yet Yentai too 'is famous throughout North China as a fruit-and-wine-growing region.' How nostalgic that in the 1970s a bottle of Chefoo wine should reach Chefoo School Malaysia, sent by the local grocer for the All Souls' Church communion table!

No more columns of coolie-draft animals . . . No crippled beggars . . . the rickshaw has given place to a motor-powered tricycle. Time and Yentai have marched together and time has brought cleanliness, hygiene, education, hospitals . . .

Churches? In 1972 when Dr Crofts visited Chefoo, St Andrew's Church was boarded up and seriously damaged. The Union Church, which had welcomed the young Chefusian faces for so many years, was undisturbed but smelt of decay — as did the Catholic Church. But 'one place of worship was in full use, its courtyard crowded with children. It was the Buddhist "Jade Emperor's Temple" on the summit of Temple Hill. It had been fully restored with bright paint and new woodwork — but it no longer served a religious purpose. Its gods had been removed from their stations and replaced with a cycle of five dioramas, using giantsized plaster figures.' In reality they portrayed a Marxist morality play which brought down wrath on the exploiters of mankind.

Was there no trace of Christian work? Did anybody remember the CIM Schools?

Chefoo . . . or as the Chinese would pronounce it, *Dse Wu*.*

Gone? *Dse* means a rare plant which gives long life. *Wu* is a screen. Today *Dse Wu*/Chefoo/Yentai is only beginning to peep from behind its screenlike bamboo curtain. Did Chefoo ever give long life? Everlasting life? Heaven will answer that one day when Yentai Christians gather before the throne of God.

That's the name we can give to this Chefoo century: long life!

(Quotations from *Chefoo: A Microcosm of China, Old and New* by Dr Alfred Crofts, The Denver Post, 7 May 1972.)

*Schmidt, *Glimpses of the History of Chefoo, 1932*.

A bedtime cuddle at Chefoo Malaysia

AND THE WHEELS GO ON TURNING . . .

'A dorm aunty is . . .
> Someone who gives us paper at rest houer.
> She gives us toof past.
> She gives us games to play.
> She poots us in sick bay when we are sick.
> She gives us barv's.
> She tuc's us in at nigt.
> She helps us in difficult sercimstansis
> She takes us out on Saturday.
> She gives us hair cuts.
> She gets us up in the morning.
> She helps us to make our bed.'

1981. A new era, a new country, a new little seven-year-old Australian but the same name — Chefoo.

Despite communism, despite the exodus of missionaries from China, neither the China Inland Mission nor the Chefoo Schools died. Instead, they spread themselves, like the fanning tail of a peacock, to the twenty million Chinese plus many millions of Indonesians, Thai, Filipinos and other peoples living in south east Asia.

So in the early 1950s, ex-China missionaries and scores of new recruits who had never seen China's shores began to arrive in the Far East. The China Inland Mission wasn't really the right name now for a group working in many countries of East Asia with a headquarters in Singapore. It was possible, though, to be the same mission under a new umbrella. The name Overseas Missionary Fellowship spelled a depth of meaning to members new and old, but many folk even in the 80s think of the mission still as the old CIM. And, indeed, some supporters in the home countries never really knew that OMF *was* CIM.

Nine hundred missionaries people OMF today. From all over the world they have gone to settle in Eastern Asia, in places as remote and far apart as Japan and Korea in the north to the islands of Indonesia on the Equator. Pippa lived with her family in Central Thailand where her father was a busy doctor at the mission hospital. Gillian's parents worked in Hong Kong as part of Christian Communications. Little Christine lived in Taiwan where her father was a church planter among the tribespeople. David's father was a university lecturer in Java. Rick's father was in administration in the new International Headquarters in Singapore and Gareth's mum and dad ran a Bible College in Malaysia.

1881's problem had surfaced again. Where could these children get a western education? International Schools were springing up in the Far East now but the fees were astronomical — having children educated there was not normally a financial possibility for missionaries. Neither did these schools cater for children going home to a variety of countries. If the alternative was to return home for the sake of the children's schooling, not only would OMF lose valuable workers but the nationals would be left without their Bible teachers, church planters, competent medical staff and so many others.

This diagram shows how the Asian countries where the parents had settled formed a natural circle, like the rim of a bicycle wheel — a circle with no hub for the children.

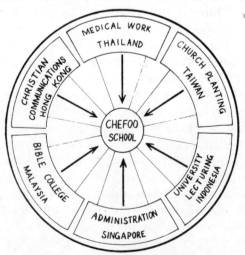

History began to repeat itself. Having explored the possibility of openings for OMF workers in Malaysia, Mr Williamson realized that the Cameron Highlands would be a cool refreshing holiday spot for weary missionaries — reached by a snaking road climbing five thousand feet in the jungle-covered mountains. And would it be the possible site for a school, too? At this altitude the children would be free from the sluggish tropical heat. A few pupils were already struggling to learn in Bangkok, Thailand, but here in the Camerons was there a more permanent home for them — a hub?

The present OMF holiday bungalow, situated like a castle on its own miniature plateau with a breathtaking outlook, was the first Chefoo School in Malaysia. In 1954 Mr and Mrs Guinness moved in as house parents with 24 children and two teachers. Miss Dickson held sway in the tower classroom with its peepholes behind the pictures, where gamblers fearing a police raid used to spy on the winding road. 'One lasting memory I have of her,' remembers a Chefusian, 'is sharpening pencils with a razor blade out of the window. I really was impressed with the efficient way she did it.'

'I was at Chefoo School when it was reborn in the Cameron Highlands,' another recounts. 'My memories are most happy. Yes, parting with our parents was always a tearful time but we were blessed with very loving and creative house-parents and teachers. Uncle Henry, once an MK himself at Chefoo in China, fully understood our unique situation. We received a lot of individual attention.

'My best memories are of the beauty of our surroundings and of the care given in helping us to notice them. New places for the school picnics were highlights. We spent days by the reservoir, at the fish hatcheries, up at the searchlight where thousands of moths gather and on the plateau where a cannon boomed blank shells to scare off any communist guerillas still in the jungle.

'When anything unusual occurred we were sure to have it added to our realm of experience. One night we were awakened to see the jungle, across the valley from us, ablaze. At other times we hiked to scenes of landslides or helicopter landings.

'I remember an occasion when three consecutive birthdays in May were celebrated simultaneously, yet each birthday child had his or her own table with a uniquely decorated cake and place cards to match — all hand made by Uncle Henry. I remember because I was one of those children . . .'

And 'Uncle' Henry himself, a past pupil, married in China Chefoo's Assembly Hall, a parent of a little son who went to Chefoo School in Kuling, and at that time a house-father, has this to add: 'Surely the hundred percent promised in this life,* is for both parents and children and I would like to testify that as a child and a parent this has proved abundantly true.'

*Mark 10. 29-31

Author Sheila Miller (left) and her class in the 1970s

'I remember lots of fun,' writes yet another Cameronian pupil — 'the stilts made for us to stalk around on, the "walkie-talkie" rigged up for us, the tree climbing, the "jungle gyms", the fish pond being scrubbed out so that we could use it as a swimming pool, whole day treats when we would go off to Jungle Pool and, can you imagine it — having to plunge thru a cold, yes a *cold* bath *every* morning. I think it was meant to be good for the constitution!!'

'Another lasting memory,' writes an old boy, 'was the beautiful outdoor life. Those wonderful views over the jungle, the troops of baboons who swung thru the valley one afternoon, the walks on Sundays, the fly-catcher plants, the occasional hornets and snakes to add excitement. I loved it all. Even the drains were fascinating, the way they filled so quickly in the rain storms, pushing over our hastily-made dams.'

Despite its spell, the handsome bungalow seemed to grow smaller and smaller. As missionaries took up the challenge of S.E. Asia their children needed Chefoo School. Again the scouts went hunting for property.

Just at that time the Cameron Highlands were declared clear of communist guerillas who had made the mountains' rain forests their stronghold during Malaysia's Emergency. Folk had been apprehensive of living there, but now the property market sprang to life. Again the Cameron Highlands was becoming a holiday resort for the wealthy. Beautiful houses and bungalows with panoramic views were being snapped up and, unfortunately for OMF, prices were rising.

Hidden in a little green valley was a seven and a half acre estate, known as *Lali*. It seemed, with its big main house and running stream, to be just right for a new Chefoo. The staff prayed about it but the price being asked for *Lali* exceeded the funds available.

One day Mr Hogarth, the house-father at the time, heard that *Lali* was being offered at a lower sum than formerly quoted. He telephoned Singapore Headquarters, and the directors there thought it would be wise to find out who the owner was. They were able to discover that she was an English lady who was leaving rather suddenly for

Britain and wanted to get her property matters wound up right away. The price she was asking was considerably lower than the agent had stated.

By 1959 the school was in residence — still a comparatively small Chefoo for which was erected a new long low L-shaped building to act as dormitories, dining room and classrooms.

Very soon Chefoo, Malaysia outgrew these original buildings. Numbers crept up — thirty, fifty, eighty and, by 1970, a hundred. A hundred children now having primary education only. The world had shrunk, and distances to home countries by air were comparatively short. It seemed the right thing for the new generation of MKs to have their secondary education at home. Boys and girls from the States began to go back there to OMF hostels from which they attended High Schools as day pupils — as did the Australians in their homeland. Chefusians from Britain went home to boarding schools and used their hostels for holidays only.

By the time Centennial Year had dawned, parents had the opportunity of choosing to send their children to a large American Christian school in the Philippines, which has also started to cater for British children by introducing an 'O' level course. So at the age of eleven the Chefusians scatter — most to their various home countries, some to Faith Academy in the Philippines, and a few to international schools in other big cities of the East.

And to achieve this, Chefoo has come alive with children's buildings, teachers' residences, a tennis court, a netball court, a playing field, a small swimming pool and a long curving driveway inviting all who love CIM and OMF to come and rejoice in the Lord's provision for these MKs.

The hub had become a reality and, because it was there in the centre, Pippa's, Gillian's, Christine's, David's, Rick's and Gareth's parents could continue working with the varied peoples of East Asia — at the point where the rubber meets the road.

Gone the sound of breakers on a North China shore; gone the ocean-filled summer days and gone the biting cold of winter when icy winds hurled themselves across snow-

Chefoo Malaysia today

covered Siberia to penetrate the dormitories and classrooms of Chefoo. Weihsien, Kiating, Kalimpong, Shanghai, Kuling and Bangkok — all only memories, too. But
the school now still lived in a little valley where perpetual
summer scattered with cool rainy days made life sing like
the tropical dawn chorus and noisy cicadas.

The international staff is hand-picked by God from
English-speaking countries world-wide. Sixteen in all:
seven on the home side, seven involved in teaching, plus a
nurse and a housekeeper. The school syllabus has been
compiled by teachers from USA, Canada, Britain, New
Zealand and Australia. The aim is to teach a child what he
ought to know by the age of eleven in his own home
country.

The standard is high. Academically the children have
been able to make the transition well, from Chefoo School
in the Far East to secondary education at home — as well as
and often with greater ease than any contemporary from a
primary school in Manchester, Chicago or Sydney.
Educationalists, parents and pupils themselves have
written appreciately of the training given at Chefoo.
Perhaps this is partly due to sets of excellent text books by
companies who publish material suitable for both North
America and Britain.

'In maths I remember,' recalls one now grown up, 'we were in different groups according to nationality. I always wished I could do American maths. It looked so much more interesting!' Since then, of course, Britain has experienced the changeover to decimal currency, which has taken much of the headache out of shop bills!

As school television programmes aren't available, a wide and profitable use is made of films from different embassies, supplementing text book material. Another feature, especially in Social Studies, is teaching the skills of research. The Chefusians learn where and how to find information in their own classified library. One old boy of Cameron Highlands days sent the school a gift. 'Please buy library books with the money,' he wrote, 'because it was at Chefoo I learned my love of reading.'

Malaysia is rich in resources so Social Study lessons are peppered by visits to tin mines, oil palm, rubber and tea estates. A highlight for the top class, in their last year at Chefoo, is a week-long cultural trip to Malaysia's capital city, Kuala Lumpur. No one can forget that week even though sight-seeing takes place in temperatures in the nineties!

'KL is a stifling sauna with onion-tower roofs. Congested traffic is jostled along by crash-happy drivers pulsing their way inch by inch to their destinations,' was ten-year-old John's impression.

Alan managed to describe his visit to the Zoo in rhyme — from an unusual point of view:—

ZOO ANTICS

I opened my mouth to let in the cool,
And slid nearer and nearer the edge of the pool,
My body propelled like a torpedo released,
My actions were fast for my being was greased.
To the opposite bank I slowly drifted,
Like a champion swimmer who's greatly gifted.
Basking, sunbathing I lay unafraid
Waiting to halt those who tried to invade.
Sliding 'mongst reeds and resting my pride,
Trying my hardest not to collide,
Living in splendour and much glory too,
Spying the children, who came from Chefoo.
I fell asleep dreaming of days
When I once did learn about crocodile ways
And then I remember the pranks I did hear
When trying my first time to catch a mouse-deer.
But my dad, he got caught, and then my turn too,
And now I am here in this boring old zoo.

And Kevin was intrigued when the teacher took them to the Houses of Parliament:—

'Strolling into the Senate Chamber, we heard the guide explain to us that after a bill is approved in the House of Representatives, it arrives here in the Senate and goes over to the King. Also, here in the Senate the King sits, perched up on the highest seat, overlooking the great hall. Up at the other end we were asking questions about this. "That is where the King sits and that is the public stand," I heard the guide explain.

Edging closer, moving cautiously nearer to fame and wealth, here I was. Should I do it? Yes, I said to myself. I did it!

I was on the seat of fame, overlooking the great hall, perched up there on the highest seat, feeling all important. Two cushions — whheeezzeee — Wow, I leapt off. This chair wasn't made for my type. I joined the group quickly. But for a split second I was King. Think of it — Yang di-Pertuan Agong Morris — King of Malaysia.'

The Level Sixers were not the only fortunate folk to visit the capital. One day, in the seventies, an invitation arrived at Chefoo for two British teachers to attend a garden party in honour of Her Majesty Queen Elizabeth II. The excursion stirred the imagination of all. 'Dear God,' whispered one Chefusian on the night of their departure from the Camerons, 'bless those two miserable offenders, Miss Goodall and Miss Edwards, as they go down to see the queen. (Pause) What are "miserable offenders" anyway?'

Although the wording of the 1662 Anglican Prayer Book was very beautiful, the Chefusians began to use their own new little Church service book more frequently!

All the same the eavesdropper to one little conversation would have expected a fuller concept of Christianity from these two Chefusians:

Angry girl to boy: 'You'll never be a Christian when you grow up.'

Boy: 'I know. I'm going to be a carpenter.'

At one stage too during a 'flu epidemic, when Sick Bay was packed, it seemed that it might be necessary to know all about the life to come. 'People keep going to Sick Bay,' observed one. 'They go in but they don't come out.'

That same little ward, gay with Uncle Ned's Peter Pan, Pooh Bear and Pluto painted on the walls, saw one little boy approaching the school nurse for treatment on his spots. 'Please Aunty Kathleen,' he said, 'I want anointed.'

Sick Bay at Chefoo School, Malaysia is a busy place but the unwell children usually pull through despite this little boy's worries. 'Aunty, I think I'm falling to pieces.'

'Why?'

'This is the second tooth I've lost this week.'

And another who was suffering from laryngitis whispered by way of explanation, 'I was in the bathroom and my voice fainted.'

Snake bite kits are always readily available but, good to relate, they hardly ever have to be used. God's protection of this little valleyful of MKs is very wonderful.

However, a-day-in-the-life-of-a-headmaster quite often included the slaughter of a poisonous pit-viper. Such an incident prompted nine-year-old Robert to write:—

HISTAM'S DEATH
Histam slid (carefully hid)
To the wood pile.
Single file, ran his body,
Till he saw a fat brown mouse
Histam gulped it down,
And nothing heard his sound.
To a room he slid,
No frown now
Was on his face,
He hadn't been found.
That night he curled
In a satisfactory world
Of his own.
In the morning he heard,
A sound and a word,
     And more,
A yell was produced.
And a few second later,
     A man!
Big and burly,
With a stick that was thin.
The stick was raised
And he was grazed.
So soon he was dead, his
     world all ended.

Yes, as well as the harmless yellow-bellies and mountain racers, it is common to see the bright green pit-viper, the banded crite and occasionally even the cobra.

Butterfly-catching is quite another story, bringing much delight and pleasure.

'One of the first things I had to learn at Chefoo even at the age of seven,' writes a Cameron Highlands' old boy, 'was how to catch and set butterflies. Virtually everybody in Aunty Ann's dorm knew the techniques backwards and I soon mastered the delicate skills of laying the thin strips of greaseproof paper gently over the wings to enable us to display the full beauty of the creatures. The dorm frames sporting our collections were a constant source of price to each of us and adorned the walls above our beds and play areas.

'Saturday morning butterfly-catching trips often highlighted the term. We made our way down the mountain to the sparkling waterfalls. I can still remember the sense of awe and excitement when a Rajah Brooke would swoop down the stream, wings glinting and glistening like emeralds, and more often than not gracefully dodge the numerous hungry nets that rose to greet it. Malaysia boasted more than eleven hundred species of colourful butterflies compared to the fifty odd species in the entire British Isles.

'Even at Chefoo, we amused ourselves for countless sunny Sundays by charging after Red Helens and Albatrosses from the tennis court, down across the playing field and up into the tree house and among the honeysuckle blossom next to the stream, with huge nets like giant white flour bags streaming from the bamboo rods in our hands.'

One sunny day, a teacher, marking books in her classroom, overheard a conversation outsider her window.

'I've just seen the most beautiful female,' one boy said to another.

With a certain amount of consternation, she glanced from her window to see which girl had just passed by. Both boys were carrying butterfly nets!

*   *   *

The vision of the Christian church spread northwards in the minds of the new missionaries. Some early mission stations were so far from the equator that OMF decided to operate a small Chefoo School specially for the children of missionaries in Japan. In actual fact Chefoo School, Japan, was already on its feet before the Malaysian Chefoo got going! It started in December, 1951 — with one pupil and one teacher. So there was even a tiny Chefoo in existence to finish off 1951 after the exodus from Kuling in the spring. As the little school grew, Miss Taylor and Miss Nicholl taught the children in Karuizawa, a holiday resort in the mountains.

Miss Taylor was almost unique in her long association with the Chefoo Schools. She herself had been educated in North China and after tertiary education at home in Canada, had returned to her old school in the 1930s to teach, eventually sharing in the experience of internment. When the school was located in Kuling after the war, Miss Taylor was there too. Now here she was in Japan!

In 1953 the little school moved to Sendai, half-way between Tokyo and Aomori on the island of Honshu, but as the building there was almost falling apart they were soon stirred up yet again.

The Fellowship had been looking for the right place for the school because a generous friend in England had given money, earmarked specifically, 'For a Chefoo School in Japan'. By 1963 the cash was available, the need was apparent but the property was elusive. The city of Hakodate in Hokkaido, Japan's northern island, had been chosen as a possible location. A number of places were examined but none seemed suitable.

'There's one more property I know of,' said the estate agent, 'but it's out of the city at a little place called Nanae.'

OMF decided to have a look all the same.

It turned out to be an orchard with grape vines, several varieties of apples, two cherry trees and pears. An old farmhouse nestled near the gate which opened on to a small side road about a hundred yards from the main highway to Sapporo. The price was reasonable. And so OMF acquired the new Japan Chefoo.

A few years later it was discovered that the land had greatly increased in value — in fact, it was worth four times what the mission had paid for it. Their Heavenly Father must have been planning on this lovely spot for His children, within their resources — plenty of play area, an abundant supply of grape juice, apples and other fruit to enjoy, with the bonus of the beauty of blossom in springtime. And then — the view, far across the plains that varied in their colour with the seasons and stretched out to the blue mountains in the distance. About half-an-hour away in that direction was Onuma Park, the lake there dotted with tiny islands.

One red-letter day in April, 1964, something special happened for the new miniature Japan Chefoo. That day, a stone inscribed

'To the Glory of God
Overseas Missionary Fellowship
April 21, 1964'

was on view. Later it would be set into the wall by the school front entrance. A little ceremony was led by the architect. A director unveiled the Foundation Stone and dedicated the building to the glory of God and the education of the children of missionaries. The group of visitors with the eighteen children then sang their great song:

'Lord of all power and might
Who art the Author and Giver of all good things,
Graft in our hearts the love of Thy name,
Graft in our hearts the love of Thy name;
Increase in us true religion,
Nourish us with Thy goodness,
And of Thy great mercy, keep us in the same,
Through Jesus Christ our Lord.
Amen.'

Although the money donated was so generous, economy prevented installing a teachers' toilet. What came to be known as 'a Sabbath Day's journey' had to be undertaken to the far side of the building! One day, however, a new gift arrived for Chefoo Japan and it was set aside for the desirable addition of a staff bathroom. At last the necessary facilities were installed, the procedure assisted by many a small Chefusian's prayers, interest and curiosity. During the evening devotional time, when all was ready, the house parents were barely able to hide their mirth as one small intercessor thanked the Lord for the teachers' 'new little house. And, please God,' he added, 'help them to use it well.'!

'We used to have a really great attic at Nanae,' remembers a Japan Chefusian. 'All us girls would play house up there for hours at a time and then there was a basement, too, and we put in endless hours roller-skating.'

Snow makes life full of fun in the winter — much to the envy of their Malaysian counterparts! Ski-ing, sledging and the riotous activity of building igloos. Real cold outside but, says one, 'really warm and friendly with a lot of love,' inside.

Evening devotions at Chefoo Japan

215

And the guardian angels hover over Nanae in the same way as they do over the little green valley in the Camerons and as they have done over the Chefoo Schools of China days. A rather unusual and dramatic instance of God's care was obvious when an earthquake hit Japan's north island. It was near enough to that precious little school to bring disaster to Hakodate University, only ten and a half miles away, yet left Nanae undisturbed with neither damage nor injury.

Chefoo children there are the same living, learning, looking-for-love, giving-love youngsters that have peopled the schools through the century.

'Fold your clothes, Malcolm,' said Miss Weller in an effort to keep yet another dorm tidy.

'I don't fold. I muck,' replied Malcolm.

'You'll see the results of your work in twenty years' time,' Mr Welch of Chefoo, China days encouraged one of the teachers when he visited their new school.

'Twenty years!' thought Mary. 'That seems almost a lifetime!' Yet today, she knows a fine young officer in the US Navy who was once a Japan Chefusian. Another has graduated in optometry, really loving the Lord and seeking His will for her life. Yet another has qualified as a nurse and attended Ontario Bible College. Trophies . . . due to lives invested in back-up-role missionary work for the Lord . . . but more than that, due to the investment of the Saviour's life for them. And they realized it.

*   *   *

The dedication of *Green Gables*, Tagaytay, Philippines, in 1954, marked the beginning of yet another Chefoo School in South East Asia — only a small beginning with seven children but a beginning marked by God's 'wonderful works and thoughts' towards them.

In those early days of Chefoo, Philippines, the children lived on a ridge 1,800 feet above sea level with a magnificent view of Taal Lake and its volcanic island. The school led a chequered career after that, with small schools in Calapan, Manila and Baguio City high in the mountains. Eventually, as in Malaysia, the cool mountain

216

site was found to be the best, and in 1970 the school was reopened in Baguio, 5,000 feet above sea level. This was no little village as in Peninsular Malaysia but a university city where every bend in the road revealed hundreds of houses nestling into the mountains. And yet Baguio City was also a holiday resort in the island of Luzon, 160 miles north of Manila.

At first Chefoo occupied a house which was adequate for the school. And then something entirely new happened! So many would-be missionaries were joining the Fellowship from the continent of Europe that it seemed the right thing to open a German-speaking section of Chefoo. A new venture indeed! Where? How? What about extra space for the German-side classroom, a bed-sit for the new German teacher and a small dorm for the continental children? Yes — a second house was needed. Yet it seemed a pity to separate the two sections of the school and deprive the children of extra international playmates. And besides, the new house just had to be near so that staff could come and go easily, especially in the rainy weather, of which Baguio has more than its share.

OMF looked around the area but nothing turned up. The building next door had been a student boarding hostel and the new house father approached them about the possibility of renting it. Oh no — that would not be possible at all!

One day . . . (the words start such exciting sentences especially in God's stories) the owner of the property next door happened to be up in the mountains. And the staff member in charge 'just happened' to meet him. Yes — he found the owner most interested in renting his house. Permission was given to make an opening in the wall between the two gardens so that it wasn't necessary to use the two front gates when going to and fro. In addition the area beside the school had been cemented just a couple of months previously, giving a good playing area which did not get muddy in the rainy season.

When one girl was at school, memories like this were stored in her mind. 'I remember the baseball games,' she

Chefoo Baguio

says, 'climbing trees, going for long hikes and skit nights. The atmosphere at Chefoo, Philippines was always lively and exciting because of the many different personalities. Truly there was never a dull moment. At one time there were five girls in the classroom and one boy. We all had our turn of falling in love with him! But seriously, the friendships I formed there have made the strongest ties I have to this day. Some friends I haven't seen for ten years but I still correspond with them. It seems like years never make a difference and you can just carry on from where you left off.'

In fact, on that subject one China Chefusian states that their 'Round Robin letter' is still circulating the world fifty years after they graduated from Chefoo!

Ken went to Chefoo, Philippines in 1970. 'One week while I was there,' he recalls, 'a typhoon hit us. It was so wet and windy outside that we weren't allowed out of the house for four days. At times it was quite frightening and after it was over, we drove around and saw all the damage it had caused.

'One educational trip I shall never forget was a visit to the gold mines, where we saw the whole process from the ore coming in by train to the different metals that were extracted. Then we saw them refining the gold in a furnace and pouring it out into ingots. We were able to hold the small sample ingots that they made for testing — the large ingots were still too hot to touch when we left.

'Looking back, I realize how my time at Chefoo stands out. I can remember vividly lots of the things I did, compared with the years before or after.'

Well, Centennial Year marks the end of this lively little Philippines Chefoo. A few years ago the school was re-formed for German-speaking children only. Now the directors have decided that these children would benefit more by attending Swiss and German schools in Singapore. A good home to act as an OMF hostel for them has just been found and already Chefoo, Philippines joins the happy list of memories stirred by words like Shantung Province, Kiating, Kalimpong, Shanghai, Kuling and Bangkok.

'The Chefoo atmosphere,' says Miss Taylor, 'no doubt has some connection with the natural beauty of all these surroundings — marvellous beaches, blue, blue sea, a view of snow-capped Kanchenjunga, walks through wooded hills and valleys bursting with birdsong, fresh mountain air in the midst of the tropics and seasonal delights in the north but, of course, it's much more . . . One of my contemporaries (as a pupil) — an only child who had long separations from her parents, started an essay on Chefoo with this statement, "Chefoo is a lovely, happy place" and that *joie de vivre* has been characteristic of Chefoo wherever it is. The secret is that it is a Christian school.'

Matthew chapter 18 reveals something special on what the Lord Jesus thought about children:— 'At that time the disciples came to Jesus, saying "Who is the greatest in the kingdom of heaven?" And calling to him a child, he put him in the midst of them and said, "Truly I say to you, unless you turn and become like children, you will never enter the kingdom of heaven. Whoever humbles himself like this child, he is the greatest in the kingdom of heaven. Whoever receives one such child in my name receives me . . . See that you do not despise one of these little ones; for I tell you that in heaven their angels always behold the face of my Father who is in heaven."'

(verses 1-5 and 10 & 11, RSV)

'And calling to him a child, he put him in the midst . . .'
Central.

The China Inland Mission and the Overseas Missionary Fellowship have tried to do just that. They have kept their policy on missionary children central in their thinking — a hub, as Mr Arnold Lea, one of the directors, so aptly described Chefoo.

But by itself the mission could not carry the responsibility of the hundreds of children who have graduated from Chefoo. That is why God gave prayer partners to the schools. Thousands in the homelands have brought the mission's children to Him in prayer. Teachers, dorm aunties, parents, grandparents, uncles, aunts and friends worldwide lift the little green valley in Malaysia and that beautiful 'orchard' in Japan up to the Lord. Surely Chefoo must be one of the most prayed-for schools in the world.

No wonder God blesses the Chefoo Schools. No wonder a Chefusian from earlier in the century could say, 'Every time I hear or see "Chefoo" something lights up within! My experiences of Chefoo bring to mind a story-book-English-boarding school. But, of course, our atmosphere was different because of Christ.'

The reason for this is not just because there is a hub with its spokes radiating to so many East Asian countries on the rim of the wheel. Rather the answer lies in the whole bicycle. Out ahead is the front wheel — the missionaries themselves in the forefront of the battle for God — but without Christians praying as a back-up force — the back

The Lord in Control

MISSIONARIES OUT FRONT

SUPPORTERS BACK HOME

PRAYER

THE CHAIN LINKING CHRISTIANS
BACK HOME TO GOD'S POWER

wheel linked by the chain of prayer to the source of power, the Lord Himself who is in control — no progress could be made.

In the early days of the new Cameron Highlands Chefoo, a series was running at Morning Assembly on the life of their founder. Using graphic flash cards, the teacher was bringing alive the fascinating details of Hudson Taylor's teenage years — before CIM was ever born.

One small boy in particular was captivated by the great goal in Hudson Taylor's thoughts. He was a non-OMF child, from a Roman Catholic army family. Not only at Assembly time was he absorbed in the story but also during class hours. Later in the Woodwork Room, the teacher there was conscious that he was muttering to himself as he busily sawed through a piece of wood. Intrigued, she drew alongside and heard him mumble, 'Wonder if that bloke ever got to China.'!

CENTENNIAL HYMN FOR CHEFOO SCHOOL

Thankful friends from far and near,
Celebrate this joyful year,
Chefoo born on China's shore,
Grown through days of peace and war;
Lessons learnt in class, at play,
All have led us in His way,
 Hearts and voices let us raise,
 Our *Jehovah-Jireh* praise!

Now in highlands valley cool
Worldwide prayers surround our school,
Fears and laughter, tears and joy,
Love for every girl and boy.
Crafts and skills and half-term fun,
Inward battles fought and won,
 Guide and Guard through all our days,
 Our *Jehovah-Jireh* praise!

L.S. Conway.

St. George's Windsor. 3rd verse descant by L.S. Conway

Thus rejoicing, let us still Serve our Lord with mind and will, Having gained this

hundredth year Strong in faith we'll perservere. Staff and students

Staff and students from each age / glorious

Glorious heritage Though all else be sacri — ficed, We'll REMEMBER JESUS CHRIST.

Share this

heritage

Well — yes, he did, as this saga shows. In June 1981 the schools are celebrating their Centennial Year. To mark the occasion the new General Director, none other than Dr James Hudson Taylor III, himself a Chefoo China boy, and the great-grandson of 'that bloke', is addressing the children in Malaysia. They sit, in their centennial T-shirts — listening, absorbed, thrilled with their heritage. Above the stage hangs a long red banner with beautifully lettered script, appliquéd in white by a creative dorm aunty. In just three words it sets the tone for all that has happened at Chefoo throughout the century. It is their special motto: 'Remember Jesus Christ.' And they've done just that.

A hundred years old today. Happy birthday, Chefoo.